Michael H. Kushniru

SHATTERED PANE

JKS Publishing

This is a work of fiction. The events and characters described herein are imaginary and are not intended to refer to specific places or living persons. The opinions expressed in this manuscript are solely the opinions of the author and do not represent the opinions or thoughts of the publisher. The author has represented and warranted full ownership and/or legal right to publish all the materials in this book.

Shattered Pane
All Rights Reserved.
Copyright © 2015 Jenna K. Scott
v2.0

Cover Photo © 2015 thinkstockphotos.com All rights reserved - used with permission.
Interior Illustrations by Michael A. Rosario

This book may not be reproduced, transmitted, or stored in whole or in part by any means, including graphic, electronic, or mechanical without the express written consent of the publisher except in the case of brief quotations embodied in critical articles and reviews.

JKS Publishing

ISBN: 978-0-578-16063-4

Outskirts Press and the "OP" logo are trademarks belonging to Outskirts Press, Inc.

PRINTED IN THE UNITED STATES OF AMERICA

Dedication

To my mother, *with whom I shared this nightmare side by side. Words of advice, anger, and inspiration flowed freely from your lips; helping me to heal from each event which occurred. I am the luckiest person alive to have you to back me up in whatever problem happens. Life is life, good or bad, we still have to find a way to make it through. She has been my inspiration, support, healer, friend, and Mother. Her belief in me has helped me to heal and recover; not only from those who have hurt me, but from the mistakes I have made on my own.*

Thank you, for giving up your dreams to help me fulfill mine. It is a gift I will never forget. I love you more.

National Suicide Prevention Lifeline
1-800-273-8255

National Child Abuse Hotline
1-800-422-4453

Chapter 1

The Beginning

My entrance into the world started one crisp, bitterly cold morning, on January 22nd, 1972 as the infant daughter born to Wade and Shay Scott in Broken Arrow, OK. I was given the name Jenna Kaci Scott, but my nickname quickly became Kaci. My brother, Gage, was 22 months old at the time of my arrival. At almost two years old, he was rambunctious, full of energy, and hard to manage. Adding a newborn to the family was a difficult task. Young parents of two, trying to juggle a newborn, full time work, and manage household chores; left my parents with little time for anything else.

Obviously, I don't remember a lot from my early years, but I do recall a few happy memories. We lived in an olive green trailer in Enid, Oklahoma, down the street from my maternal grandparents, Greg and Eden Brawl. Our trailer was modest, affordable, and an acceptable place to start our lives together as a family.

Gage was an adventurous, bold two year old with a temper. Whenever he would get mad or upset, he would run away. He always ran straight to Grandma Eden's house. Safety was not a concern. The dirty gravel road had only a few residents on it, and they all knew Gage was there. The lot in which Grandma Eden's trailer sat, was a dead end road. Mom could watch him safely reach his destination from the kitchen window. His appearance was always announced ahead of time with a simple phone call from my mom, telling Grandma Eden to be on the lookout for a temperamental toddler again.

I wonder if we appeared to be a normal family in those early years, with two loving parents and doting grandparents.

Did people who knew us have any idea of the horror our twisted futures would bring? Were we the family who neighbors waved to in passing, but never stopped by because we were "a little off"? Probably not. Secrets as dark, and disturbing as ours stayed well hidden. A curtain of security had been closed off to naive outsiders.

As soon as my parents saved enough money, they bought three acres a few miles away from Grandma Eden's trailer. It wasn't long before they began building our house. They would sit me on the main floor as a toddler, and allow me to hammer nails into the floorboard. My dad started the nail, as I pounded away with my little hammer. I loved being out there with friends and family alike, building our future home. It was fun, lively, and full of action. I loved the feel of scratchy patches of floor board under my legs; the slightly abrasive wood tickled my skin. Small memories, but good ones.

My mother was slender, with thick, shoulder length curly blond hair. Her bright blue eyes and slender nose were beautiful as she would look into mine with a soft lovingly gaze. Her face felt smooth to the touch. It was long and thin, with just enough filling to be pleasing to the eyes. She has always been a beautiful woman, lips of thin pale pink, smiling at me as we Eskimo-rubbed our noses.

My dad was tall with rich dark, straight hair. His eyes were dark brown, so dark, they looked black when he was angry. His face, and nose were round and full. He was incredibly fit, with strong wide shoulders. It seemed as though he could carry the world on his shoulders without a hint of struggle. The work crew was quiet and laid back, yet noisy

SHATTERED PANE

at break times and lunch. It was a safe, peaceful atmosphere.

Dad was a carpenter by trade, and designed our house. I remember it with crystal clear clarity. I was safe in that house. I didn't know it at the time, but it would be the only home in which my childish innocence was intact. We lived there until I was seven years old. It was a ranch with a two-car garage, and a walk out basement. The house was set back from the road, with a huge front yard, and an enormous back yard. It had been cleared of trees and shrubbery, as it stood silently alone in the middle of our property.

Yellow and pink were my favorite colors, they flooded the earth with the bright cascade of warmth and happiness. They made me squeal with delight as their bright auras danced through the air. Sunshine and flower's made life simple, easy, and carefree. The colors of my happy soul.

They chose a yellow paint with pinstripe brown accents for the exterior. The front and garage door matched perfectly with the brown striped outlines. The perfect house to hold our perfect family.

Walking in the front door, the dining room and living room were open, just a half wall to separate them. It was the perfect 'round about for a hyperactive toddler and a barely walking infant. We rolled around on the orange and yellow shag carpet squealing with delight, ignoring the rug burns our knees and elbows had acquired.

The kitchen was just passed the dining room were we sat down for meals served at a small, four-seat wooden table; perfect size for our young family. Meals were cooked on our old fashioned yellow metal appliances-the kind that lasted forever.

I had a picture-perfect little girl's princess room. It was painted a light pink with a pearly white twin size bed, centered on the wall across from the door. I could see effortlessly out the door at night, and know my parents were there. I always slept with my dolls, Barbie's and stuffed animals. I loved having them with me. They kept me safe, and warm at night. If I had a bad dream, Mom always welcomed me in their bed. She would lift the covers, and mold my body into hers as if we were two matching pieces to a puzzle.

Mom liked having our rooms close together so she could peek in at night, and see her babies sleeping peacefully. I spent countless hours playing in my room with my dolls, and toys. Mom was warm, caring, and constantly showering us with hugs and kisses. Always making sure we were clean, clothed, fed, and well-loved. She was the world's greatest mom, just like the saying on her coffee cup. The best part of my childhood was spent in that home, I wish we never left. Gage and I were best-friends; he was my hero.

When I look back on my life as a child of five, I felt as though I was looking through a freshly cleaned, spot free, window pane. The entire world was clear as the sun shone bright upon me. Mother Nature and glory all around me.

The trees were grouped together in a crisp variety of green, off in the background behind our property. The grass was freshly cut, soft and plush under my bare feet. As I ran, the wild flowers exploded with various brilliant colors. Small fluffy clouds lay gently in the sky, floating silently, suspended by the earth's atmosphere. The smell of fresh clean air tickled my nose. Watching closely, a vast array of birds swooped overhead. Flying too fast for my short legs to keep up. Jumping my full stride just to reach out and touch one. Their wings maintaining their stride as they propelled them into a glide, easily with a hunger for their next destination.

I recall chasing the fireflies, and dragonflies at night with complete amazement as I watched their lights dance up and down. Full of brilliant colors as they would decide whether or not to stay. I danced to their lights in a joyful bliss. The aromatic earthy fragrance touched my nose as I closed my eyes; I absorbed the extraordinary world around me. My surroundings were sweet, fresh, and pure. Soft as a whisper, and gentle as a lamb. As if it were the window pane to the innocent soul of a newborn infant.

Chapter 2

Finally

G age was a climber. He scampered up and down everything. If the couch was in his way, he went over it not around it. He tried to teach me how to use my feet and hands to pull me up. If I couldn't reach, he would offer a boost with his hands on my bottom. The big problem with that was, once I got up somewhere, he would be off to another adventure, and never helped me down.

In 1977, I was 5 years old, and received what I thought was the best present in the world. Santa brought me a new bike. Of course, that year was one of our biggest snowfalls, with five feet of snow blanketing our yard! Houses, roads, and driveways where nothing but pure white. Gage and I built actual tunnels and igloos in the yard.

I was devastated I couldn't ride my bike. I was excited about the gift, and couldn't contain it. It was yellow with a few pink heart accents, and a long yellow banana seat. The handle bars were tall, I had to sit on the edge of the seat just to reach them. Mom set it up in the basement all winter so I could sit on it, and pretend I was riding free. Freedom and adventure was within my grasp. I prayed my legs would grow long enough to reach the bottom pedal before spring.

After what seemed like a whole year, warmer weather finally came; the snow melted, and Gage promised me he would teach me how to ride. That is exactly what he did. Well, sort of.

We walked my bike to a gravel road that ran downhill on the side of our yard. I saw it every day as I played outside, never really noticing that it was actually a road. We stopped at the top, suddenly it was like an enormous mountain, and I became incredibly frightened. It was the first time I remember ever being afraid of something. All I could see were the huge white rocks jutting out everywhere, just waiting for my little knobby knees to be gashed upon them. I hated the sight of my own blood and bruises, but that did not stop me. The rocks sparkled in the sun, and it was an extremely long hill. The bottom of the hill was capped off by a circle drive. I sat on the seat and waited for directions. He whispered in my ear, kicked the kick stand, and told me to head for the grass. My feet barely hit the pedals. He gave me a swift push, and off I went, but he neglected to tell me how to use the brakes. I soared down the hill at the speed of lightning. My hair slashed in the wind as screams of excitement rang from my mouth. The exhilaration was unbelievable as my heart threatened to leap from my body. I never did find the brakes on that trip, but luckily there was a nice patch of soft green grass at the end. The elation of the rush continued beating in my heart. Adrenaline ran free, and surged through my veins. I couldn't believe I just soared my new bike down a jagged mountain and survived.

Mom came from the house screaming at Gage as she ran down the hill, terrified that I was hurt. A flash of anger escaped her eyes as she shot a glance towards him. Gage ran, grabbed her arms, and told her it was okay. He taught me how to jump off before we started. She scooped me up, and checked me over carefully. I wasn't hurt, aside from minor cuts and bruises. Excitement raged through me so hard, I was in complete awe.

Mom apologized to Gage, who was kicking at the rocks remorsefully, head hung low. He loved me as much as she did, and would never intentionally hurt me. He wanted to help me ride my bike. I didn't care about any of that. I was amazed from the sheer excitement of the ride. As my courage and skill grew, so did my love of riding that bike. The faster the better. It gave me many days of pleasure, and would later provide a means of a quick adventure.

Gage and I were always together. If we weren't riding bikes or climbing trees, we were playing on the simple metal swing set in the backyard, sometimes all day and into the night. I loved swinging the most. I flew high and free, without a care in the world. Gage, like a monkey, climbed on the set, and pushed my swing as high as it would go. He shoved me down the slide to see how fast I could go. I loved every single minute of it. My behind was constantly bruised from landing with a firm "thump" on the dirt at the bottom. As soon as I landed, I scrambled back up for another turn.

Mud pies and castles were built after a long drenching rain. Being dirty, muddy, and scraped up was a normal part of our childhood. I never paid much attention to the scratches, and muck sustained from good clean fun. Mom or Gage could fix anything wrong with a kiss, a Band-Aid, and a hot bath back then.

Our closest neighbors lived two acres to the north. They had a girl my age. Her name was Sue, and we quickly became friends. Her parents owned horses and ponies. I would go to her house, and work in the barn with her and her dad. We shoveled poop, helped wash and feed the animals, and giggled like silly girls the entire time. We rode horses in the field between our houses; our hair whipped in the wind, the sweat glistened on our horses' powerful bodies as we urged them on to go faster and faster. Riding bareback on one of the horses or ponies gave me a taste of complete freedom and excitement. The air was so pure, we basked in the sunlight, and let the horses set our course.

I felt tension between my parents. My mom worked long hours at the plant, and my dad was home a lot due to the lay-offs or bad weather at work. Mom wasn't home during the day to take care of breakfast or lunch, but I guess we got along fine. I do remember the dinners though, especially her homemade ham and beans. My mom cooked as she did laundry, and cleaned the house. She never had a moment to sit down, and relax.

My dad wasn't around a lot in the evenings; when he was, he smelled of Old Spice, beer, and sweat. I never remembered him working much, but I knew he had a job. Money was a constant issue. My mother worked far from where we lived, and worked a lot of hours. She put us in day care so she knew we were taken care of when my dad worked, and most of the time when he didn't. Dad wasn't nearly as attentive as mom was, and mostly left us to fend for ourselves. Gage wouldn't go to daycare without me. He would climb as high as he could in the play room, and cry until they brought me in for him to see and hold.

Although my dad didn't work much, he was rarely home. I never knew where he went unless he was in the garage working on the car. I know he worked side jobs; sometimes they lasted until late into the night. It became easy to notice when he'd come home drunk. His staggered walk, slurring words, and the loose use of curse words gave it away every time.

Dad's mother, our Grandma Fran came from time to

time to help my mom clean and cook dinner, but she was never friendly. She was tall, and overweight. Her bulbous nose fit her full cheeks and lips. Her skin had moles and skin tags. She loved to fry foods, I always thought she looked as though she'd been burned from the grease splatter she cooked with. I don't remember her being a welcoming presence in our house. Her mood was short and sharp; I can't recall her smiling or pulling us into her lap with the intent to tickle or play. I think helping around the house was her only way to feel like a part of the family; it was the best way in which she could manage. Even though her temper was short, I still loved her being around.

Dad's father, our Grandpa Eli, was diabetic, blind, with his toes amputated. The doctor's removed more as his circulation decreased. However, the diabetes never stopped him from drinking his beer all day. I never saw him without one. I remember him in his wheelchair, which made him seem short. He was a little overweight with a balding head, and a sad full face. He seemed completely vulnerable, as if he had given up on any dream he'd ever held.

Chapter 3

More Needles

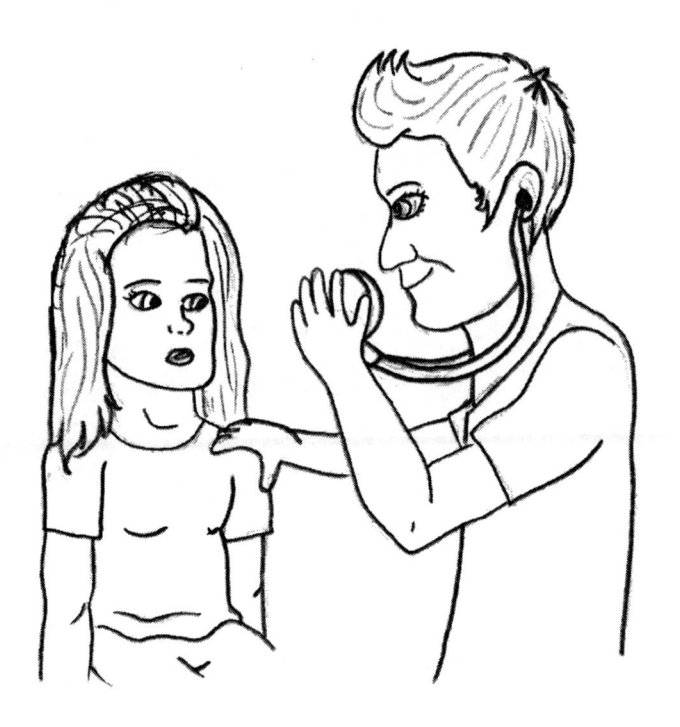

Grandma Fran died from a heart attack on my brother's birthday. Dad told us the day after, so Gage wouldn't have that memory embedded in his mind each year--like a bad gift that could never be returned.

Grandpa Eli stayed with us a lot after that. He was unable to care for himself due to the blindness, and the loss of his legs. My mom took over his daily living needs. Mom cooked, kept him clean, and always made sure he had his medicines. His insulin shots were the worst part for her. Between working, taking care of the house, us kids, and caring for Grandpa Eli; she was always exhausted. I don't remember my dad ever offering to help. She never let that stop her from smiling though. Her face always shared her beautiful smile.

The only time I remember her doing something for herself was when she and Dad invited my Aunt Simone and Uncle Baron over. They would play cards around the kitchen table after tucking us in bed. The sound of their laughter trickled down the hall, and into my room. I was too curious about the jovial conversation; it was too much of a temptation for me to be with my mom, so I usually snuck in, and lay on the floor under her chair with my blanket and doll. Eventually, I fell soundly asleep at my mother's feet. Sometimes Mom would hold me in her lap, with my head on her shoulder, and played her cards around me until I fell asleep. Gently and quietly, she would lay me in my bed, and tuck the covers tightly around me.

My mom's company also sponsored a co-ed softball team. Mom and Dad were both great at it, so they joined in on the fun. We did as all the other kids did-- ran around, and played happily on the park equipment as they whooped and hollered at their teammates.

Grandpa Eli was not the only one who struggled with illnesses. I had asthma and allergies, not just the run of the mill seasonal stuff; the *race to the emergency room when I turned blue* kind of asthma. The doctors started me on allergy shots. My mom took me to the doctor every few days to get them. Those days made life harder on her. The forty five minute drive to the doctor took up precious time that she didn't have but she made the time because she had to.

That routine went on for a few months. Then she convinced the doctors to let her give me shots at home. She had experience with Grandpa Eli's diabetic shots so they gave her the training, and supplies to administer them herself.

My mother's parents, Greg and Eden Brawl, moved to an older sub-division in Oklahoma City. Grandma Eden was a strict Catholic, worked at the hospital as a nurse's aid, and was at church on Sunday without fail. It seemed like she prayed every second she had. She said a lot of beautiful rosaries, using them as part of her night time routine. Grandma Eden held the patience of a saint, always looked for the good in people, even when there was only a tiny shred of goodness to be found.

Grandma Eden believed in helping people when she could, and took in foster children whenever possible. Most of the kids stayed for only a short while, but there never seemed to be a shortage of children hanging around the house. Daniel Dole stayed the longest. Daniel, Gage, and I became close friends.

Their home was older, and developed problems so they decided to build a new one. Our whole family banned together to build a house in Stillwater for my Grandma Eden and Grandpa Greg. They both retired, so they welcomed the peace of the country forty-eight miles away, secluded from the hustle, and bustle of the city.

They used oak trees cut from the property, and meticulously shaped them into the precise size that was needed for the four outer walls. Grandpa Greg was particular about how things should be done. He had his own idea of the right or wrong way to do something, and had no qualms about letting a person know it. Especially when it came to his kids.

Grandpa Greg bellowed directions, and guided the guys on how to cut the correct angles. He wasn't shy about pointing out imperfections either. He towered over the blueprints, with fierce conviction on his long full face. His eyes were ice blue, his nose long and thin. His lips were small and tight whether he smiled or not. His hair was thin, gray, and was combed back, as if he were trying to make it look fuller. He was tall and fit for his age, shoulders wide, full of power.

Grandma Eden was always a wonderful sight. Her average height and slender body matched her exquisite blue eyes and short, brown, and wavy hair always perfectly arranged. Her skin was always clear, soft, and smooth to the touch. She had just enough wrinkles to give her a grandmotherly appearance. Her slender nose would twitch with a smile as she watched us play, and she loved on us constantly.

The family crew often worked late into the night. My cousins, my brother, and I watched or played while it was being built. We mostly climbed trees and played hide and seek during the daytime. The house was surrounded by top-notch climbing trees. The higher we got, the better, and there were some tall trees. Most of the cousins could get high enough to see the whole of the property that spanned several acres.

I scampered all over finding the perfect hiding spot for hide-and-seek, and found a great place where no one would ever find me! It was in a tree that was exceptionally tall, thick around the trunk, and had limbs that were spaced apart at the perfect distance to accommodate the reach of my little arms. Three limbs sprouted close together at the trunk, then opened up just a few feet away from it to form a hollow space (the perfect size to hide a little girl). The branches extended up, and converged together like they were all vying for the sun's attention. That tree became my special place to go hide when Gage or my cousins got cocky in the game, or when they made me mad simply, by being boys.

When the last nail was hammered, and the decorating was done; what emerged was a gorgeous, log cabin surrounded by exquisite natural beauty. The air smelled of fresh saw dust, and tasted of hard working sweat. The two story cabin sat back, away from the road, and was one of a kind; with the pure natural cedar log walls, and an old wood burning fireplace in the living room. The simple aroma of pine and cedar always tickled my nose.

The front porch expanded the length of the house, and there was a porch swing that hung from the rafters. There was an incredible view, the air was always light, sweet, and fresh. An old fashioned concrete white horse and carriage was set in the lawn. Grandma turned it into a flower garden, and planted small purple and pink flowers in it. The gravel driveway held enough room for all five of their children, and their families to park.

The trees closest to the house were neatly trimmed about six feet up. Few cars passed the house, leaving only the sights and sounds of nature on most days. The windows were new, clean, and received sunlight with not a single dark spot to block its warm glow. It had all the outward appearances of being a dream home, where the family that created it would be safe, and untouched by the world.

Chapter 4

Cabin Fever

Our family had it all: a close bond, friendship, and spiritual gratitude. We were all at Grandma Eden and Grandpa Greg's cabin most of the time. I was happy when we were there. I had no reason to avoid the cabin then. Grandpa Greg would get out his little green riding mower mounted with a bright yellow seat. He would attach the small wood carrier on back, and give all the grandkids a ride. Each of us would have a turn to drive. The exhilaration of being in control of such a huge tractor left all the kids begging for turns. The adults stayed at the cabin and talked. They caught up on each other's lives, and relished in the exquisite cabin which they had built. Sometimes they would play games; other times they simply fished or hunted.

I loved to sit around and observe the family. Searching their features and wondering what their hopes and dreams were. My mom was the second born of the five kids. My Uncle Garrett was the oldest; my grandfather made over. My Uncle Landon was the third. Grandma's blood ran through his veins. My Aunt Sara came fourth. She was always small, and seemed fragile to the touch. Uncle Randy was the baby. His hair was strawberry blond, he was always meticulously cared for.

Our family would all come out with their spouses and my cousins. We would laugh, talk, and play together while the adults were busy fishing or hunting. On the days they hunted we were sure to see a deer strung up to a tree and gutted for that night's meal. It was a natural process for the grandkids to witness, and no one ever got squeamish about the blood.

All the women worked together to cook a huge delicious

feast out of whatever was killed first. I was taught from an early age how to shoot a gun, and that deer and turkey were at their best when fresh. Fresh meat was always tender, and highly desirable in our family.

Family photos were taken frequently. I would barely turn-around from one flash, before another would blind me. The little horse and carriage was the staple of many family photos. My little cousins, especially McKenna, loved to sit and pretend to ride. Her attraction to it was remarkable.

There were many things going on in our family. My mom's family was happy and enjoying life, while my dad's family was falling apart. Between Grandma Fran dying and Grandpa Eli's need for constant care, it was hard for them to work together as a couple. My mom was working long hours, my dad's lack of employment, and his endless drinking; took a toll on their marriage.

My parents informed us they were filing for divorce. I didn't understand at the time what they were telling me. All I knew is that we were moving out of the house. Mom and Dad would no longer be living together. They both promised they would love us, and be there if we ever needed them. Mom took custody of Gage and me.

My mom told us the house would be sold, but the small amount of money they split wouldn't get us much. It sold quickly, and Mom hadn't found a place for us to live that she could afford. She left for two days; I was never sure where she went or why. I just assumed she needed some time to work things out for herself. We stayed with my Dad while she was gone.

When she returned, we packed our belongings and

SHATTERED PANE

moved into my Grandma Eden and Grandpa Greg's house. After we were in and settled, I felt as though I was living a fairytale life, with a superb forest surrounding me with pure beauty. I often wonder if my Dad ever fought for us or offered more money, so that we didn't have to move in with them. If he worried or mentioned any apprehension.

Grandpa Greg was so happy we were there. He could hardly contain his enthusiasm as he wrapped me in a soft baby blue quilt, like a cocoon. He put me on his lap like an infant, while he sat and watched the news. I think it was the only program he watched. It felt good, safe, and it was special "Grandpa Time". I felt special to have this little moment of peace with him. He would explain what the news was talking about, and answered all the questions I asked. Each evening Grandma Eden would bring him his medicines, and wait as he swallowed them with a glass of milk.

When my mom wasn't working, she and Grandma were usually in the open kitchen cooking or canning. I could watch them if the news became too boring. Sometimes I would simply join in on the process to help pass time in the evenings. Gage always lost himself in the property that surrounded us. He was either fishing or scouring the woods for trees to climb. He also made friends with the neighbor boy, Shane, who lived a few acres to the south of us.

Grandpa Greg shared stories of his childhood; the manner in which he was raised, and the war he fought in. My Great Grandfather Brawl was a strict Baptist Preacher. He raised his children to believe in God, fear His wrath, and follow the righteous path using the Lord as their ultimate leader and destroyer. Following His words exactly as written in the scripture. Grandpa was sure to mention this whenever there was a controversial issue on the news over a religious matter.

His time in the war was difficult. Even at a young age I could read his face. I remember thinking how hard it must have been, recalling the few events he shared. Reliving the nightmare he had gone through, the anguish and terror he felt. The horror shone blazingly as his eyes glazed over during his descriptions. He was hit in the head with shrapnel, and was discharged as a wounded warrior.

We played little games on the couch, easy ones that he could remember. Mostly thumb wrestling or itsy bitsy spider, as our fingers climbed the web together. He read me books, and told me fairy tales. He could be descriptive at times; he was good at creating the scenes in my mind. The images he described were clear and precise.

Together we would sit for hours on the back porch, watching Gage as he caught fish. We praised him for the big ones, and begged him to save the little ones. Grandpa Greg always made sure it was always stocked with tons of fish to catch. Gage loved fishing in that small pond. If I was out there with him, he would help me with the bait, and the fish I caught. Gage was an amazing older brother; he chided and teased me as normal siblings do, but he was always there for me.

Grandpa would tell me how beautiful and special I was to him, not like the other grand kids. I meant so much more to him, I was his favorite. I had to keep that a secret from my cousins, they could easily become jealous. It made me feel special and loved. He would kiss my cheek with a tender and loving grace. My heart raced with joy and exhilaration.

SHATTERED PANE

We sat on the front porch swing at night as Grandpa told me about how the moon would come into position or change its shape from one night to the next. Stars shone bright, the constellations could easily be seen with exact proportion. We talked about many things; shared our different opinions on this or that, as the stars and clouds held all our conversations in complete confidence.

Sometimes it was chilly in the evening, the air held a crisp bite to it, and Grandpa would rub my arms to warm me up. If my feet were cold, he would put them in his hands, and gently rub them to restore my circulation. I could hear and see Mom and Grandma as they smiled at me through the screen. They loved watching Grandpa Greg and I so close.

It was incredible that he would do these special things for me because he loved to pamper me. He took special care of me, and always made sure I was comfortable. It was gentle and soothing. I felt special, safe, and perfect.

Soon after, he began to kiss my cheek, the top of my head, even my neck and ears if my head was turned just right. Each kiss was soft, and smooth or they would come with a tickle I hadn't expected. He shared with me that rubbing and kissing were as important as life itself. It made humans grow healthy and strong. I loved his gentle caresses. They were warm, soft, and usually put me right to sleep.

Chapter 5

Grandpa Eli

My father moved into my Grandpa Eli's house. It was a forty five minute trip from the cabin. He had visitation rights every other weekend. We played games, climbed trees, or sat on the back porch, and talked about school or whatever was going on in our lives. There was a full backyard to run and play in with a meticulously clean tree line at the edge of the lawn.

There were times Dad took us to the baseball games, played catch with us, or took us to watch the airplanes come in at the airport. He always had something planned for the weekends we were there. Grandpa Eli carried on, he was still drinking beer, and added Alka-Seltzer to his daily routine. My dad took over his daily needs; it was difficult, but necessary.

I can remember the house like it was yesterday. My Grandma Fran must have loved green. Every wall inside and out was painted with various colors of green. The bushes lay neatly along the front walk, and the grass was always freshly cut and trimmed. To the left as you walked in, the drapes and couch matched with an ivory and vibrant red floral print. The couch sat right in front of a huge picture window. The sun would shine in the window incredibly bright, the dust and lint softly floating through the air. I could easily reach out and grab a handful, but when I looked, my hand was empty. In the air was a smell of mustiness, and I could feel the tightness all around me. My dad's room was right off the living room with sparse decoration or personal items. We usually shared his bed at night due to the fact that the couch was incredibly uncomfortable. Its cushions were lumpy and uneven.

The back of the house held a small porch with a wooden wheel chair ramp. The kitchen was small; it felt cramped and cluttered. There was just enough room for Grandpa's wheel chair to round the corners. He would grab ahold of the table and counter to maneuver himself around. Every movement he made was accomplished through touch. It was remarkable watching him feel his plate, silverware, and necessities. Food portions were given in a clock format, so he could determine where the food was on his plate. It was fascinating to watch. I was amazed at how blind people could function somewhat independently, if not completely on their own.

My Uncle Baron and Aunt Simone were my Godparents. Simone was my dad's sister, they had one son, Mike, who was older than Gage and I. They would visit on the weekends we were there. Mike threw the football as we fumbled, failing to catch it. Croquet was often set up; the whole family would participate. It was fun and full of laughter as we would grill outdoors on the bar-b-que pit. Family recipes were made inside to go with whatever main dish was chosen for that day.

A short time later, Grandpa Eli died, leaving us with only one set of Grandparents alive. Losing him was as sad as Grandma Fran's death. Guests shed tears and held each other out of comfort and need. It was sad, as he laid in the coffin. Fake makeup cleared his once patchy skin tone. Hands crossed over his belly as if he was simply taking a nap.

Chapter 6

Lip Sync

My Uncle Garrett and Aunt Paige had come for a visit. The weather was perfect. My uncles took turns caring for the issues around the house so Grandpa Greg wouldn't have to. There was usually some small thing that needed a healthy man's attention. Grandpa wasn't getting any younger; some things were difficult for him to do. Aunt Paige took this time to sit and visit with us catching up on everything she missed.

On this night, Mom and Grandma Eden went outside to say good-bye. They were not gone long. As usual, I climbed onto Grandpa's lap snuggled in my blanket. He started stroking my arms gently as he usually did. That comfort and serenity was a wonderful treat.

Then he placed his hand under the blanket, and traced his finger along my panty line. His hand gently glided across my belly and over my nipples. I told him that those were special, private places. My mom told me only she, and my doctors were allowed touch or see them.

He informed me he was a special person. He always made sure his grandkids were growing healthy and strong, as if he followed this guideline with all my cousins. In his mind it was the right thing to do. He didn't push or go any further.

He did that again the next night while Grandma Eden was cleaning the upstairs, and then again the next while my mom was in the cellar. It never lasted for longer than a few minutes. I told him over and over again they were private areas. I quickly scrambled off his lap, letting him know sternly I didn't like it, and it felt wrong.

One night, out of nowhere, he grabbed my face hard, and ruthlessly slammed his lips into mine. I felt my lip crack as his tooth made contact. He forced my mouth open with his tongue and fingers. The sting of my split lip left the taste of iron as the blood reached my tongue. He tasted like onions; his tongue was slimy soft. His lips were wet, crushing, and cold. The power behind his mouth was harsh as his tongue stiffened in my mouth, hard and fast, gagging me to the point I couldn't breathe.

When his grip loosened from my face, I ran up the stairs to bed, completely confused as to what just happened. That minute felt like an eternity. Later I learned it was called a "French Kiss"; I didn't like it at all. I couldn't wait until first grade started; less time with him suddenly seemed like a good idea.

A few nights later, Grandma and Mom had gone downstairs to put grocery items away in the cellar. It was time for bed; I didn't want to be around Grandpa, so I made sure I was ready. I had begun a routine of keeping my distance from him. I started wearing my robe, but it was getting too small. I didn't feel completely covered.

As I ascended the staircase, Grandpa called out my name. I froze and looked his way. He reached his hand out softly, and apologized for scaring me. His apology seemed sincere; I longed for his gentle warmth. He promised that things would go back to normal; he wasn't happy with himself, and was ashamed of what happened.

He asked me to watch the news with him. Hesitantly, I sat with him; but I stayed on the far end of the couch, out of his reach. He seemed lonely, sad, and old. I felt a little sorry for him, after all, he did apologize. At almost eight years old, I still held the hopeful heart of a child who doled out forgiveness easily, especially for this person I had come to love and cherish.

Not long after I was seated, he reached over hastily, forcefully, and hurtfully once again. He used his left arm to shove me back into the couch, the harshness of his elbow knocked the air from my lungs, and crushed my ribs. His face was twisted with a need; sweat covered his skin. I fought hard, pushing his sticky body away. He pulled my nightgown up, and shoved his other hand straight down my panties. His fingers were rough and calloused as his long jagged nails clawed at my private areas. I couldn't move at all. It happened so fast it didn't seem real. He thrust his fingers between my legs harshly, his mouth crushed my lips as his "kiss" kept me from making a sound.

When he released me, I struggled and ran. I told him that I was going to tell how he hurt me. He whispered harshly that no one would believe me. He quickly convinced me that it was my fault. He told me I was a slut. Apparently, my long Wonder Girl night gown made him crazy. I should never have worn it. The robe was no help. He was sure to let me know that if Mom or Grandma found out, they would beat me with a belt strap. I had only been spanked once before by my dad. It was horrible and embarrassing. My mom never hit or hurt me. I don't know why, but I believed him.

I was crying and didn't know what to do; my brother was out catching fish until dark, and there was no one around to help me. I couldn't run to the cellar to find solace in my mom so I ran up to the bedroom and cried. I was upset and confused. I didn't understand exactly what just happened. I felt completely betrayed. My heart burned as my body trembled from fear and shock. My private areas throbbed, and bled from his nasty intrusion. My window pane was swaying; a storm was coming, and it needed to be braced.

    I spent the night in a fitful sleep. I was petrified he would follow me. My mind could not understand the magnitude my body just suffered. I wanted and needed his warmth and love back. Instead I was paralyzed with fear, guilt, and embarrassment. I wasn't sure what I had done so wrong that would cause punishment from Mom or Grandma. There would never be special time with Grandpa again.

    Eventually, I drifted off to sleep. I was taunted the whole night, as the scene from the evening flashed behind my eyes. My head was trying to find a reason for the betrayal and pain. The violation was one my mind could not comprehend.

Chapter 7

Painful Display

I tried so hard to stay away from him after that. I was hurt, and my stomach was sick when I saw him. As he sauntered by me casually, the foul smell of sweat and the taste of blood would rush to my mind. Unfortunately, he didn't care. I avoided his path daily; he became angrier, more verbally hateful knowing I was deliberately keeping my distance. Horrible names I didn't understand were constantly spit at me as he told me I was nothing but "his" whore and slut. I was the devils spawn created especially for him.

Grandpa was incredibly sweet and gentle when someone was around. He threw hateful glances my way when no one was looking. Not even a hint of the madness which stirred inside him was revealed to the family he loved. Gentle kisses and hugs were given to my cousin's as they came to the cabin. Smiles and laughter filled the air as he would tickle them or pretend to chase them. I missed the times he did that with me.

He followed me everywhere I went, making sure I knew I would never get away. No matter what, I would always be within his reach. Threat after threat flowed from his mouth. If I tried to run or deny him, he would explain how he would torture my mom using a hammer to drive nails into her eyes, or slowly peel her toenails off with pliers. He made sure I knew he would, and could, kill my brother in a hunting accident or by drowning him in the pond. He was definitely stronger than any of us, and I knew his temper all too well. I never knew what to do to stop him, I knew any choice I made would be a nightmare for all of us. I felt as though it was me fighting against the Devil himself, disguised as an Angel in white undershirts, which made him seem so innocent and incapable of harm.

Hiding was always difficult. Grandpa was like a canine. He could smell my scent anywhere I went. His threats continued as he showed me different tools, and gave full descriptions as to how he would use them to hurt my family. Each time he showed me, the torture was something different. Those vivid images overtook my dreams, slowly destroying my plans for the future.

Grandpa Greg always had his own room, straight upstairs on the other wall. His snoring and restlessness kept him out of Grandma's bedroom. Grandma Eden and Mom shared a king size bed; Gage and I shared a bunk-bed all in one huge room at the end of the second floor hall. One night I used the restroom. When I finished, I could see my room on the left, and I checked Grandpa's on the right. I headed slowly and quietly back to bed. Out of nowhere, a hand grabbed me by the hair, the other shielded my mouth before I could utter a sound. I fell as I was being dragged backwards. The carpet burned at my heels; I was choking from lack of oxygen, couldn't see who was behind me, and didn't know what was happening. It felt as though someone was trying to break my neck or choke out my last breath. I heard the door close slowly as I fought. I was in Grandpa's room. I resisted his tight grip, until he stopped me with strikes to my ribs from his fist, forcing the air out of my lungs. His hushed laughter rang deep in my ears, as he watched me gasp for air. He slammed his head behind my ear as I fought against his agonizing grip. The pain was searing hot; it left me dizzy, and dazed. My heart beat pounded loudly in my ears; the horrible headache, and overwhelming fear paralyzed me. I was afraid and unprepared for what would happen next.

SHATTERED PANE

His free hand clumsily yanked at my nightgown, and he unforgivingly tore my panties off. I felt the gash they left, as he did this in one quick pull. My knees were ripped apart as he quickly, and awkwardly, rammed his manhood into my privates. The force of the split brought excruciating pain while his hand concealed my attempts to scream. I felt my flesh sting as he bit my shoulders and nipples until they bled; always using his hand or mouth to keep me quiet. The searing pain ravished through me so hard I couldn't think; I just continued to fight as hard as I could.

The weight from his body crushed the air out of me and split through my ribs where his punches had landed. I could feel the panic overtaking my body and mind. His breath was horrid; his breathing hard, hot and fast. I felt the wetness all over my face as he panted, and licked my skin. My head was spinning as my privates were violently ripped and torn. I could feel every slash within me at each movement he made. Fast, hard, and agonizing. I searched the room for something to use as leverage; all I saw was the deep seeded hatred and fiery anger in his eyes. His face mangled in his desperate need to punish me. My legs were forced back into my chest as his pelvis slammed into mine. It felt as though my legs were being torn off with each hard, deep thrust. His mouth crushed mine as he bit, and tore at my tongue and lips.

He didn't stop until his release; I could feel his body shudder on top of mine. It terrified me. There was a sticky wetness and severe bleeding between my thighs. I was petrified, and didn't know what came next. As quickly as it started, it was over. He shoved me off the bed, I landed painfully on the hard, cold floor. He told me to never tell anyone, that he would slowly kill my family, making sure I was there to witness, and hear their screams of anguish. I didn't care about me I had just been tortured, but I was petrified for my mom and brother. After what just happened, I was sure he was capable of doing unfathomable things to them.

I slowly tried to stand, but the searing pain in my thighs wouldn't hold me. I slowly crawled, as the rough carpet beneath me burned my skin. Sore and bloody. I made my way to the bathroom. Six feet felt like ten miles. I could feel thick blood dripping down my cheek. Each agonizing inch I moved was met with pain and blood. Droplets of it tingled as it streamed down my legs. I stopped it with my nightgown so no trace would be found in the carpet. I had to protect my family from a fate worse than mine. I used toilet paper to clean as much blood off as I could. I rinsed the sticky blood, and wounds off in the sink. My hair was tangled, bloody and matted. After rinsing it with water, I carefully brushed it out. Every stroke was met with a sharp sting.

I was thorough, yet quick as possible, fearful that he would once again come from nowhere. My head, privates, and nipples were covered in wounds as I made my way to the dresser for fresh pajamas. I could never let them see me like that. I climbed the bunk and into my bed, hiding my bloodstained clothes under the sheets and between my legs. I would have to remember to throw them away the next day. I kept my body pressed as close to the back corner as possible in a futile attempt to protect myself, and the sheets. I thought sleep might never come. I rested a moment, as I watched and waited. Slowly, I drifted off into an unwanted, disturbed sleep.

SHATTERED PANE

When the alarm went off for school the next morning, I found it difficult to move. My body throbbed, my ribs were sore, my thighs bruised, and I had a horrible, sharp headache. I was sick to my stomach over the horror from the night before. When Grandma came to make sure I was awake, she instantly knew I was sick, and chalked it up to a virus. I cleaned up my head wound the night before, and kept it facing the wall. They kept me home from school that day. Mom went to work, and Grandma had errands to run; so they asked the neighbor to come over, and watch me even though Grandpa was home. I quickly fell back into a fitful sleep.

Chapter 8

Promises Kept

Alice was my sitter for the day. She was a sweet older lady who lived next door. When I woke up, I quickly slid by grandpa's door to the downstairs bathroom. Careful to not make a sound. Alice did not know I was awake, and walked in on me while I was using the restroom. She saw the blood between my legs. The bleeding continued through the night. I was so exhausted; I thought I could clean it up before anyone would notice. She was surprised, then suddenly relieved--I wasn't sure why. She went to the pantry to retrieve a big pad, and a wash cloth. She told me to take a shower and she would get me a fresh set of clothes. She taught me how to place the maxi pad. It was horribly embarrassing, as she tried to explain the menstrual cycle to me. She changed the sheets on my bed, brought me some Tylenol, and tea to soothe my stomach. Grandpa was relieved when he heard that I started my period. In his disturbed mind, he was off the hook for the trauma he created. Now he didn't have to worry about leaving me a bloody mess.

My mom called her gynecologist, and questioned them about starting my period at such a tender age of barely eight. They explained to her it was possible, and that it would most likely be inconsistent until I hit puberty. That eased everyone's minds. I did start to bleed off and on, sometimes for days on end. My belly, back, and privates hurt constantly. Whether it was from him, or if I actually started my menstrual cycle, I was never sure.

The rapes continued time and time again. I learned to not use the restroom at night. If I couldn't wait, I checked his door to make sure it was closed tight, and used the restroom downstairs. If I used the one downstairs, I wouldn't have to turn my back on him, and I could see if he opened his door to wait for me. Most of the time I was lucky, and avoided him, but a few times he caught me in the hall. When he did, he grabbed me from behind. I knew what was coming, and prepared myself as much as I could for the brutalizing punches and blows. It didn't take long before I never turned my back on his door. Instead, I watched it with every step I took.

I wouldn't heal from one event before he would catch me again. It didn't matter where I was, he would always find me. My vaginal walls could not hold his girth. I could hear the skin tear and feel the sharp sting as he plunged in and out. Always leaving me ripped, and intensely sore for days to come.

If I went outside to play, he would make an excuse, and leave through the front door. He knew all my favorite spots, and would scour the woods until he found me. I would climb different trees when I saw him coming. I would pretend I was a chameleon as I tried to hide high in the thick branches, and green leaves. I always said no, and tried to run. He was always bigger, faster, and smarter than me. With the ground covered in sticks and bugs, he would violently rape me again--leaving scratches, and bruises as his weight pounded me into the ground.

Grandpa had an uncanny knack for hearing things, despite the fact that his ears were so bad. Occasionally, Grandma Eden asked me to go to the cellar to find stored food or replace items she bought. He would find a way to meet me in the cellar, and continue what he deemed as "God's" punishment for my sins. I felt the weight of my sins each time he got to me. Even when I relented, he was still harsh, whispering horrible names and threats in my ear. He always managed a strike to my head, back, stomach or ribs. It was his way of letting me know that he held the power. His whispers of threats, and ghosts always left me feeling vulnerable, and exposed.

Sometimes, Grandpa would sneak past Grandma and Mom's bed, cover my mouth, and snatch me from my bed. He was quiet as a mouse. I learned to stay as closed to the wall as possible with blankets, and pillows to shield me. Sometimes I would crawl into bed with Gage or Mom, claiming I had a bad dream. They didn't know I was actually living a nightmare.

One night, I heard him come in to snag me once again. Lucky for me, I just climbed in bed with Gage, and backed myself to the wall. When he checked my bed, found it empty, he retreated hastily. I was relieved and slept incredibly well that night.

Early one Saturday morning, while everyone slept, I felt the need to escape. My mind was so confused, my body broken, I just wanted a little freedom. I knew I left quickly enough, to not be followed, leaving only a note that said I was out playing. The fresh morning air was crisp, cool, and refreshing to my body. Running fast, I went to my secret place, making extra sure I was not followed. I had come to my secret place a few times before, and felt comfortable with the security it held. It was fun. I felt free-and alone.

I used a fallen oak tree as a balance beam, and lay my doll securely in the branches to watch. The coating on the tree was dark brown with few slivers of bark. Moss was growing around the tree, which left a slimy path to follow. As I ambled over the top, my footing was unsure, and slippery. Everything was wet, covered with condensation from the cool night before. The trees were tall, shaded and whistled softly in the wind. The sun shone brightly above me, leaving the world cheerful, and vivid. It felt as though I could hear the Angels from above singing softly around me.

The ground growth was high in areas, trees were everywhere, and the unblemished ground left only small trails of squirrels, rabbits, and birds. I felt completely secluded, and easily allowed myself to become overly confident. I closed my eyes while crossing the log, picturing I was in the city; balancing on the hand rail of a rusty bridge, any step could be my last.

When I opened my eyes, I saw him. I was paralyzed with fear. Neither of us spoke a word, staring sharply into each other's eyes. I dropped to my knees, my breathing stopped, and my heart felt ripped from my body. He found me, and my spot. I would never be free from his grasp. Slowly, he moved closer, one step at a time, as I awkwardly backed away. My body felt as though it weighed hundreds of pounds, not the fifty it actually was. My heart throbbed loudly in my ears. The ground was muddy, and uneven as I grabbed footholds in the terrain. I was cornered by a gathering of trees. I strained to run while slipping in the mud. My tennis shoe snagged on a branch that jutted out from a tree, tripping me, so that I fell hard to the ground. There was nowhere to run, nowhere to hide.

Instantly, he was on top of me, talking loudly in my ear as he held me down. Assuring me that screaming would do no good. Slowly pulling my clothes off one layer at a time-- he laughed loudly at my scrawny battered body. His ultimate conquest. Alone, free, and overjoyed at the seclusion we were in. My body was naked, I trembled from fear, the cold ground, and knowing what he was capable of. Birds dashed wildly away at the commotion, scared from the thumping, and voices on the ground. One hand held me down, as the other tied my right wrist with rope to a small tree. It was useless to struggle, but it didn't stop me. I wriggled to get free, and screamed as loud as my voice would carry. He let go with his right hand, and slowly scoured the earth until he found what he was looking for. He brought it closer so I could see.

I didn't want to look. I closed my eyes tight, listening to the small animals scurry around us. My back was torn as it was wedged between two trees. His sweat reeked, his words were vulgar, and I could feel his cold wet hands as they ran over my body. I tried to control my panic. He slapped me hard on my stomach, plummeting my mind back to reality. He pulled my head around so I could see what he held in his hand, a thick branch, broken at one end, with long, sharp roots at the other. The bark was rough, clinging to the sides, with stubbles from the branches it once held. Mud was caked to the bottom where he pried it from the ground. I was horrified by what I saw.

Slowly, with his free hand on my chest, he forced my legs apart wide with his knees, and vehemently jammed the sharp clawing branch roots inside me. A blood curdling scream tore from my throat, it was unbearable. Agonizing pain shot fast, and scalding hot throughout my small body. The initial entrance tore the lips of my privates all the way down. I grit my teeth, and made myself breath. Counting the inhales in my mind as I went. Concentrating on one number at a time as I used my free hand to scour the dirt, searching for anything that would stop him. My fingers only felt small twigs, and tiny rocks that I could not scrape loose, finding nothing to help. The rough bark clawed at my inner walls, the broken branches sliced through my tender skin as I screamed out in anguish, and begged for him to stop. My nails bore into the loose rocks, willing them to come free. I wanted to throw them hard, and fast directly in his eyes. Without warning, he pulled it out, it was covered in my blood and skin. Blood was streaming from my private areas. A sense of painful relief flooded me, he was done.

I looked up at the sky, it was a pale blue, not a cloud in sight. The tree tops swayed with the gentle breeze as it blew steady on this hurtful day. The smell of nature was all around. I waited patiently for the sweet pure air to reach my lungs. The pain flooded my body, but eased a bit with the branch out.

He watched me for a moment, but I would not look back. I could hear the zipper as he unbuttoned his pants, and pulled them to his knees. Tears burned my cheeks, I sobbed, and thought my torture was over. I never looked at him. My eyes clamped closed. He used all his strength as he shoved himself in, pounded hard, and eventually shook over my body. His sexual need was finally fulfilled.

Stories of the woods spouted from his mouth, as though he had become possessed. He whispered silently of the ghosts who haunted these woods. How they would terrorize the living humans until the fear triggered their targets death.

SHATTERED PANE

They roamed the earth silently, searching for their next victim. The prey who was as lost as they were.

The wobbly window pane of my soul popped with a loud crack. The fracture slowly screeching from one corner to the next. My mind gently reached out, as I ran my finger down the deep crack. I watched as the blood slowly trickled down my fingers, and onto my hand. This piece could never be fixed, the huge crack had holes in it which would always remain, and remind me of this day. The mangled glass would never seal correctly again. The wound ran deep into my inner core, my reality of life itself.

Tears flowed freely as he gently clothed me. My arms, and legs were weak from the horrid defilement. He picked me up, and threw me over his shoulder as if I were a sack of potatoes. He told me he was tired of my defiance, and rude behavior toward him. He said it was time to learn a lesson quickly. I screamed as loud as I could, begging for help that would never come. I knew where he was taking me; I knew what was in store. He promised me, if I ran from him again, the punishment I would endure. I sobbed, begging for him to put me down. Swore I would never tell. He continued on, we were close, and I was petrified.

He pulled me off his shoulder, and held me over a wide ravine. I couldn't look down. I already knew what was there as I could hear them in the slight breeze. The promise to drop me in there had always been just idle threats. I pleaded with him to take me home; I would never run again. His hands released my body as I fell, in a straight descent, about five feet down. Slowing as my feet slid between branches, and a dirt wall. My body stopped quickly on the downed trees as I landed in a tangled knot. He told me before of all the different snakes the ravine held. He described their nesting areas, all the holes on the ravine's walls which held different types of snakes, I was terrified of them. Before now it had just been a promise he never kept, that moment it was my worst nightmare come true.

The branches were full of snakes as they slithered, and squirmed to get away. They hissed at me trying to protect their nests. I could feel the coldness, hundreds of them, wrapping around my legs as I danced, losing all rational thought by the second. Panic stricken, I grabbed at the small branches dangling out of the wall, frantic of the million snake holes the ravine held. Heads popping out, hatred hissing for the intrusion I made. The tiny roots I grabbed, broke on contact. Panic overtook me, I felt as though I was losing my mind, I couldn't calm my heartbeat, I couldn't tell if it was branches, mud or snakes that surrounded me. I screamed, and begged for him to help me, but he was gone. He had left me in hell.

Mom's face flashed before my eyes. I couldn't let him get to her, I had to stop him from hurting her. My head was spinning, with nothing solid to pull myself up with. Gage was out there, alone; I climbed like never before, as I grasped and clawed at the mud to free myself. One step at a time, reminding myself of the danger my mom was in, and finally heaving my body over the top. My body laid on the ground as I struggled to fill my lungs with air. I trembled uncontrollably, and inched my body away from the horrible, nasty reptiles I just escaped.

The long walk home was terrifying. I swatted at my legs, I could still feel their bodies slithering around me. The trees became a blur, I was unsure of the direction I needed to take. I shook violently, my feet stumbled over things I never saw, as I tried to steady my wobbly gait. Tears burned my eyes at the snap of branches, and the scurry of animals as they ran away. I sobbed alone on the path back home to Grandma Eden. Nothing around me felt real. It was a nightmare. I could not wake up.

Grandma was startled at the mess I was. My voice cracked and wavered. The scratches mixed with the mud, as the blood trickled down my body, and stained my clothes. I told her I rolled down the muddy hillside, hit a tree at the bottom, and ran from a snake. Grandma quickly started the shower, I couldn't scrub my body hard enough to erase the signs of the torturous rape. I changed into the biggest pajama's I owned, and allowed Grandma to bandage my noticeable wounds. She held me tight as I sobbed from the hurt, torment, and desperation I felt. Mom was working late, so I didn't get to see her that night. Grandpa granted me a short reprieve after that. I don't know why, but I was thankful.

The threats never stopped against my family, he knew how to keep me quiet. If he wasn't beating me, his teeth would tear into the flesh on my chest, back or my head. I never knew how hard it was to keep a secret…A secret that had to be kept to save someone else's life. I was depressed, sad, and constantly sick to my stomach. Grandma kept telling my mom how hard puberty was, especially starting that early in life.

The doctors blamed the normal stress a child can have following a divorce. Ulcers were forming in my stomach. Medicine was given but never worked. The thought of

Grandpa would cause nausea, and vomiting. My body was gripped by fear whenever he was around. I would leave any room he was in, just to control the panic which threatened to break me.

Horrific acts were like a whirlwind in my mind. I never knew when or where it would happen next. I panicked constantly when I was alone. I took showers, or used the restroom only when he was in the basement, out of the house, or when Mom or Grandma was there. I was terrified, my breathing would become fast and hard, I thought I would collapse. Panic attacks came often. No place was safe.

My mind started to shut down during those grotesque times. I gave up. I found a different place to go in my head each time he came for me. One place was a small secluded island which changed each time. Looking for things new things or items to focus on. The island held trees that were bountiful with fruits and nuts. The weather was always perfect, I could feel the cool breeze on my body, and the sand as it tickled my toes. I was alone, within my own world.

My life was not my own. I held no self-confidence, respect or self-value. I was careless, and reckless in everything I did. Taking handfuls of pills, swallowing them down with any alcohol I could find. It always ended in violent vomiting, and headaches that wouldn't leave.

The pain was real; it brought me in, and out of reality. I tried my best not to gag or vomit when his tongue hit my throat. It was hard to learn how to transition my mind. The only thing it blocked was the humiliation, and embarrassment of the moment. The torment was always intense, I would grit my teeth or hold my breath to get through it. My

SHATTERED PANE

imagination was a gift in which I was allowed to escape, even if it was only for a moment. I prayed for God to release me of my life, take me into his arms, and hold me forever.

My window pane continued to crack slowly, branching outward, making the outside world hard to see. The magnificent vivid trees were no longer in view. The flowers were a vast array of dull colors. The pane, wobbled unsteadily at the tiniest hint of a breeze. Desperately trying to keep it together. It held the only element of my soul which kept me grasping onto life itself. My window was my shield, the only protection I had from the insanity that threatened to destroy me.

Chapter 9

Delight

One of Dad's weekends, Gage had a camp out for Boy Scouts. When Gage was there with me, Dad would teach us board games, how to play poker as he drank his beer, and we laughed a lot. Those were the weekends I found safe, the weekends I could take a breath and let myself heal. It was a good program for Gage; Dad assured him it would be good for him to go.

That weekend it was Dad and I alone. Dad fixed dinner as usual. Typically when we were there, we ate eggs for breakfast, sandwiches for lunch, fish sticks, spaghetti, or hamburger's for dinner. He placed my fish-sticks on the coffee table, walked around me, and laid on the couch as I ate. We watched TV as I finished my meal.

I turned to him, rested my arm on his leg, and inquired as to which game we would play that night. I couldn't decide if it would be Poker, Monopoly, or Rummy. I was hoping for Monopoly. Gage always won, so Dad could give me pointers as how to beat him. He always had good tips up his sleeve.

Dad gently took my hand in his and gazed at it. He seemed thoughtful, distant, and sad. His hand held mine softly. Something was on his mind, yet he didn't say a word. I was afraid of the bad news he was about to share. Slowly and gently, he placed my hand on his manhood. I gasped silently as he lightly placed his hand on top, and easily pressed down.

The dinner I just enjoyed was now a sickness in my gut. Slow but sure, his hand started mine in a slow rocking motion. He pushed my palm into a rub, harder, and faster as he laid his head back with a sigh. His jeans were rough under my soft palm; warmth filled my hand as it moved to his desire; feeling a growth beneath under my palm.

Moments later, he paused; looking off into the distance as though he had a tough decision to make. The sun was bright as it glared through the window. Clouds in the sky held the heavy weight of water as a storm was slowly taking over the beautiful sunny day.

Gradually he unbuttoned his pants, brought the zipper down, and exposed his manhood. Long, round, and exceptionally stiff. I couldn't believe what I was seeing, I had never seen it up close, nor did I want to. I wondered if every man did this. It scared me to think that this is what I was here for, to do these things with men. To be the whore or slut my grandfather called me.

Once again, he placed my hand on top. He guided my hand around, so I could stroke it smoothly. His hand forced mine into a hard, firm grip as it wrapped completely around, squeezing harder, and faster until his release was final. His body trembled as his mess lurched from his body unrestricted, and trickled down my hand. It was warm, wet, and thick. Some had landed on his belly, and formed patterns on his skin as it gently rolled down his sides. His shaky hand stopped as he laid his head back. The weekend continued as if nothing had happened. Like it was just another day at Dad's house. No explanation, no apology, nothing.

That time in my life was clouded with confusion. My mind was a blur, but I remembered the automatic sexual movements easily, as though it was second nature. Memories started to mesh in my head. Between Grandpa's brutality, and Dad's mental distance, my memories lost track of whom I was servicing, and when. My mind was no longer my own.

I was grateful for Dad's distance. He was nice, didn't call

me names, or hit me to get what he wanted. For that I was thankful. I knew it was meant to be kept a secret. I was scared that if I told, Grandpa's anger would surge through him, and he would punish me in the same way.

My life was one big secret after another. Grandpa held me in his clutches. Hidden bruises, horrible threats, and constant vaginal wounds reopened. I was once beautiful and special to him; now I was ugly and defiant in his eyes. I was a creature he trapped in his own personal cage. The nice talks and cuddling stopped. All I could see was anger and hatred in his eyes.

Dad's abuse was a different type. I had no idea what he was thinking, or if this was just normal. I wasn't sure if this happened in all families or just mine. He was the exact opposite of Grandpa in temperament, yet he carried the same sexual needs. I felt as though I walked the ground with "whore" carved into the flesh of my forehead.

I can't even remember how old I was at this point; I am pretty sure it was the spring before third grade. Mom came home with some good news. She had saved enough money for a plot of land, a few acres north of Grandma and Grandpa's cabin. She was elated; she always dreamed of building us an A-frame house in the country, a safe place for us to live and play. We could be free from the chaos of city life.

She always shared her visions and dreams with me; the things she longed for, the pet peeves she hated. I recall her need for a place of our own, and the freedom she wanted. I knew she wanted to be able to live her life to the fullest, and raise us the way she wanted to. She needed to no longer feel like the victim of circumstance; the urge to regain some control over our lives. I knew things were going to be better. We would be out of his house, and he wouldn't be able to torment me anymore. I would have a new piece of land all around me that I could explore, enjoy, and hide in if need be.

They broke ground and quickly finished the basement. The plan was for us to live in the basement for a short time until we could afford to build the actual main floor of the house. The basement was mapped out to hold a tiny bathroom, temporary kitchen, one huge bedroom, and a living area. Everything was open with the exception of sheets draped to provide privacy. The steps at the front door ascended to the floor of the basement smoothly. The walls were concrete, and carpet was laid. We could live down there until Mom had enough money to build the next floor up. It never seemed strange or unusual to live in the basement of a house. We were in our own place, and for that I was excited. Decorating was not important; getting the main floor put on was. So it was kept simple, and bare.

We lived there only for a short time; I can't clearly remember how long, all I know is it felt like we lived in that basement for years. Each day added more chores to the list. We all worked even harder than we did before. It was hardest on my mom; she hammered, and nailed like a pro, always with a smile on her face. Mom knew I was unhappy, and got me a puppy to aid with the stress. He was tiny, with fluffy pure white hair, and intense blue eyes. I called him Beau. Smelling of sunshine, he was phenomenal, and I loved him with all my heart. I took excellent care of him as if he was my child instead of my dog.

I only had Beau for about two to three weeks, long enough to love him completely and unconditionally. One day, on my bus ride to school, I saw Beau in the front yard. He must have followed me out when I wasn't watching. I lost track of him as the bus continued its route and turned around. I watched for him on our way back and suddenly felt the bus hit a huge bump in the dirty gravel road. I ran to the back of the bus, only to see Beau's lifeless body lay in the road behind us. I ran up to the front of the bus. I pleaded with the bus driver to stop, sobbing hysterically. He wouldn't stop. My heart ached for my tiny friend and confidant. He just laid there, so still in the middle of the dusty gravel road. I don't know if the driver was just an uncaring monster, or if he panicked because he just ran over a little girl's puppy and had no idea what to do.

I hadn't known Beau long, but I cried all day for my loss. By the time I returned home, I was completely heartbroken. Mom was there to comfort me, and Grandpa buried him in our back yard. I was depressed, and overwhelmed with hurt as Mom tried to calm me. I listened as she quietly whispered words of encouragement in my ear.

Grandpa made it a daily routine to call me on the phone. He wanted me to come over and sadly I went. He always told me what he expected from me when I got there, and ended the calls with "my dirty little whore". I knew if I relented, my punishments were not as harsh. It left more time for areas of my body to heal.

On my way over one day, I came to the conclusion that I could not continue this way. I just couldn't handle it any more. I had no idea how to stop it. My body was breaking down emotionally, and physically. There were constant bruises on my sides and back, cuts on my head, and scratches all over.

My mom was always at work, doing what she could to make ends meet, and save money to finish our dream home. It was easy for her to overlook my visible wounds; Gage and I were constantly climbing trees, and running through the woods with the few friends we had.

The next time he called, he told me what to expect, and it was the worst of his evils. Foreign objects that constantly tore; the sting of the small whip as it would tear the flesh on my backside. Huge welts were left as a reminder when he was done. They always left me in anguish, took days to stop stinging, and even longer to heal.

This would be the last time I was going there. As I slowly walked over, I decided this time I would grab a tool of my own. I knew the hiding places for all his nasty instruments; he showed me many times, using them as leverage to keep me from sharing our secret. When I arrived, I quietly took one out, and walked gingerly up the stairs to his room.

He was so still, his eyes were closed, and his breaths were slow and deep. I thought he had fallen asleep. I was hoping he had a heart attack, and was dead. Slowly, quiet as a mouse, I inched my way around his bed to the other side of the room. The sun was shining, the window open, and the sheer white curtains flowed freely at my back.

My choice was his gun; it was cocked and loaded as I deliberately raised it to his head. I stood there silently for what seemed like eternity. My imagination was going wild over the thought of his brains being splattered all over the room. The gun wavered in my small hands. Should I take his life or mine? It should be his, definitely. Mom, Gage, and I could just run. Anywhere but here.

One thought after another surged through my head in quick little flashes. I had failed to take my own life; I resigned to the fact that I was stuck here. I believed this was some sort of lesson that had to be learned by me and me alone. He made it known many times that I was not worthy of this life. As though he believed he held the power of God in life, death, and punishment. It didn't take long to understand my death was not what he wanted, but the excitement of the punishment and misery itself.

I stood there, with the gun pointed at his head. It could all be over with the slight pull of my finger. I started to cry softly, thinking about my cousins, knowing they would never forgive me. I didn't back down as the light glistened through the window creating a bright glare on his balding head.

Little by little, his head rolled my way as his stare bore right through me. His big ice blue eyes scrutinized me in the sunlight, as if he could burn a hole right through my soul. His mouth twisted up slowly into a smile when he saw the gun. He wasn't scared, didn't apologize, or beg for his life. He instructed me to pull the trigger as if he was simply teaching me to shoot. Did he want to die or was he as miserable as I was? It wasn't possible; he enjoyed the lashings, sex, and punishments he had given to me. I racked my brain to make sense of what he was telling me.

In a slow deep voice, he recapped his stories of the ghosts which haunted the earth. How they would scare the life out of some poor soul they didn't like. He vowed to haunt me for the rest of my life. Promising to never leave my side. It would be better and easier to take my own life instead. He would always be there, watching, waiting, dead or alive.

My body shook uncontrollably, both from frightening thoughts, and lifelong misery. I started to slowly turn the gun on myself, but it was hard to move; I was paralyzed by fear and defeat. He gently raised his hand as he slowly sat up, taking care and ease to remove the gun from my hands. He gradually stood up, straight and tall, overwhelming me with his close presence. He smashed me over the head painfully with the handle of the gun. I lost consciousness, and didn't remember a thing until I woke up, bloody once again, in his bed.

I guess I resigned myself to his vision for my life in this moment, although there were many more occasions I tried desperately to take my life and be rid of him. I was tired of the agony I faced on a constant basis. I tried to believe I was here for a reason, good or bad, I wasn't sure.

My life was mapped out, taking it could lead to disaster. I needed to find a way to fight for my sanity, get away from the abuse, and learn to live my life. As a young child, it was incredibly hard to understand the transition from life to death. Being abused, tortured and screamed at, I wavered constantly on the edge of the end. It would be so much easier, but I couldn't bear leaving my mom, Grandma, and Gage at the mercy of the beast. They became my focus to live. I was the one keeping them from pain or death.

I can't remember, and didn't pay attention, but apparently Gage was keeping tabs. One day, right before Grandpa's call, Gage came in. He looked at me, and asked me why Grandpa was calling all the time. I gave him the different excuses Grandpa told me to use; from putting his clothes in the wash, fixing him food, or helping him sort his medicines when Grandma wasn't home.

SHATTERED PANE

Gage didn't believe me or any of the explanations I had given. Moments later, the phone rang. Yes, it was Grandpa. Gage told me to tell him I couldn't come today. Hesitantly, I did. Grandpa was furious, screaming at me over the phone. Gage could hear the threats erupt from the handset. He took it, and hung it up. Grandpa called several times afterwards. I jumped at each shrilling ring, but we didn't answer his calls. We ignored him. We locked the doors and windows but never answered the phone. I was scared to death he would come get me, and I knew in my heart the next time I saw him, I would endure the most severe consequences.

Gage repeatedly questioned me. With every word, I brought out a lie that wasn't plausible or realistic. I wasn't a good liar, so I told him the bare minimum. I couldn't speak the words aloud to tell him the details or the horror I was living. I wanted us to run away with Grandma and Mom when they got home-- anything to get away from him, never to be found. I begged him as he paced and checked the windows every few minutes. His face mirrored his conviction to keep me safe, at least for today. I couldn't read the harsh glances he threw my way; whether they were they meant for me, or for his hatred of the moment itself.

Mom didn't arrive home until late. He called her to us with determination beyond his years. He asked her calmly if she would sit and talk with us. It had rained all day, the showers still splattered on the roof and ground outside. Their patter was a tiny distraction for me as Gage began to speak to Mom. All I could do was to sob quietly. She sat still on the couch across from me. I couldn't find my words, so he started to recall the events of the day, the little information I shared with him.

We never finished that talk. Mom stood up, paced the room with fierce anger on her face; muttering profanities under her voice. She grabbed the shotgun, and ran out into the rainy darkness with no shoes or coat, faltering through the mud in her bare feet as pure hatred drove her on. We ran after her screaming and shouting. We slipped in the mud, and raced vigilantly, as the rain stung our faces. Between both of us, we managed to tackle her midway there. We cried as we held her down, begging her not to kill him. We needed her with us, not in jail. As the hard rain slapped at our backs, we wrestled until none of us could move. We laid there in the mud, and muck together; all of us crying. She shook uncontrollably with hatred, disgust, and betrayal. She sobbed, begging us to let her "kill that evil bastard".

Once she calmed down enough, Gage retrieved the gun from her hand, and we all slowly stood up. Mom's legs were unsteady as she shook with each step she took. We both held her; calmly and carefully we walked back to our basement, muddy, and soaked from the storm. We dried off, and changed our clothes. That is when she shared her own abuse with us. It was incredibly hard to hear. It seems we shared a common bond in the matter of sexual abuse at the hands of Grandpa. I could see all the misery he put her through; I could feel her pain in my heart. Small pieces of sharp glass escaped the pane that held it together, they landed harshly on the floor below. Pieces threatening to slice my feet if I moved a muscle. My world was falling apart; there was nothing I could do to stop it.

Chapter 10

Memories

Grandpa abused my mom from the time she was four years old until she was eighteen. She was raped, beaten, and slandered repeatedly over her childhood years. It happened with her brothers and sister in the next room, or while her siblings were in the backseat of the car. He was always mean, hateful towards her and my Uncle Landon. I wondered if he got enough satisfaction from my mother, or had gotten to others as well. For some reason, he held a hatred for them that ran deep into his soul.

When mom was eighteen she finally told her mother, my grandmother, the truth. Grandma's reaction was a misguided choice to seek council from the church. The priest and the doctors convinced her that Grandpa needed her help to enter heaven. She turned to her faith and the church for help to save her daughter. Encouraged by their words, she was determined to save his soul.

My Grandma was convinced that God and Jesus were the only way to save her. So Grandma took Mom to talk to a priest, to guide her through her turmoil. The priest informed her that she should be grateful it happened to her, and not her brothers. I wondered if anyone ever questioned them. The priest did nothing to help her, only hurt her even more; as though it was perfectly fine for him to commit incest with his flesh and blood, his own daughter. Any faith in the church my mom once held was lost.

Grandma and Mom prayed daily. Grandma prayed with more strength, conviction, and unyielding faith in the Lord. The physical abuse finally came to an end for mom. She was grasping onto the reality of her surroundings, as she learned better techniques in making friends. Grandpa Greg never allowed her to have any before. The few friends she did have were friended behind his back.

My mom and dad went to school together. They started hanging out with a group of friends they both shared. They started dating, casually at first. Soon they became close, and my dad asked for her hand in marriage. She said yes. For the most part, she agreed to get away from her dad; it was her chance to run and be safe. I believe she also loved him enough to share her life with him, to try to make it work as husband and wife. The love and kindness of a man were traits in which she was wary. My dad knew the whole story and was sure they could work together towards a new life.

They married, then he went to war as a marine. They moved several times. She couldn't move far enough away from the monster who was her father, whom she hated and cared for simultaneously. She hoped this was the best way out. After all she did love my dad, if only in the best way she knew. The childhood she survived left her with mental and emotional scars that far surpassed any physical reminders she might have. It was difficult, to say the least, to be open to the affections of any man, even her husband.

They soon discovered they had created a new life together. The tiny bud flourished within her. As her belly grew, the anticipation was extraordinary. She could feel the little life move in her, turning, and kicking to be freed. After months of excitement, they met their new son. He was wonderful, small, and gorgeous. They named him Gage Michael Scott.

When the Vietnam War was over, they returned home; she worked in a factory, and he was constantly laid off from construction. The war had taken a toll on Dad, I now

SHATTERED PANE

believe he suffered from undiagnosed Post Traumatic Stress Disorder (PTSD). It wasn't recognized then, as it is today. He began drinking every chance he had.

Horrors from the war were apparent in his eyes. Nightmares invaded his dreams, and his grasp on reality slowly slipped away. The more his work decreased; the more the alcohol increased. Another chance with a new life had been announced. My mom was pregnant with me. I believe this put him in touch with reality, as he was more driven to work.

Years later, Grandma, Grandpa, and Dad convinced my mom she was crazy, and needed help; blaming Grandpa for her psychiatric distress. They wanted to admit her to a psychiatric unit. Although she realized that she needed help; she did not want them to sign her in. She would do it herself. She wanted the power to make her own decisions, not them. She would never let another person control her life or health.

After eleven years, their marriage ended, leaving deep wounds and scars were love had once been. Their bitterness and anger took over; my dad's alcoholism was a lost battle for my mom. Their marriage had ended.

My mom told me before we moved in with my Grandparents, she had taken a trip to the VA hospital to discuss my grandfather's medical and mental state. Three doctors assured her that he was on impotency medicine, and was of sound mind. He started these medicines after Grandma shared my mom's story with his doctors, years before. Grandma kept close track of the medicines he took, making sure he was getting them at the right times each day.

Three of his psychiatrists and doctors assured her it

would be perfectly safe for us to move in. That he held no sexual desires, nor could he achieve an erection. In desperate times, the decision was made to move in. She and Grandma made a pact that I was never to be left alone with him for longer than a few minutes at a time, and only if absolutely necessary. Grandma would be in charge of all his medicines so they knew he took them at his scheduled times daily.

Grandma had an unwavering belief in him no one could understand. They tried to stick to that rule, but as time passed without incident Grandma gained a false sense of security. They saw Grandpa being kind and harmless. Grandma began to trust the doctor's proclamation of complete impotency. The rule remained in place, but there didn't seem to be a need for strict enforcement of it (at least as far as Grandma was concerned). Additionally, and most unfortunately for me, Grandpa was more than just a sneaky, conniving pervert. He had pure black evil inside his soul.

Mom wasn't able to protect herself from him as a child, and while she couldn't change the past as far as what happened to me, she sure as hell was going to see him punished for his crimes against her only daughter. Mom spoke with her family over the next couple weeks.

First, she wanted to make sure that none of the other grandchildren suffered at his hands. She questioned everyone thoroughly. Second, she wanted him punished but was unsure about how to do it legally. Grandpa called me a liar repeatedly over the next few years. It was my word against his.

My Uncle Randy inadvertently started the legal process against his dad, simply by asking a friend for guidance. His friend was a lawyer, and Randy tried to find an option that could work best for everyone. His friend was bound by law to report any crimes committed, and that is what he did.

I confided in my Uncle Randy and trusted him at this time. In my eyes he was incredibly intelligent and always had a meaningful answer to my inquiries. He was a man, but yet I felt comfortable with him. The things he said always made me feel better. He spoke as though I wasn't a slut or whore, that Grandpa just had a mental illness. I finally had someone I trusted to confide in, so I didn't have to hurt my mother over and over again. That is, until my mom told me about a conversation between her and Randy.

He claimed it hurt him deeply to hear the accusations I made against his father; he could no longer bear the burden. I was invited to visit, but only if Grandpa was a topic I would not discuss. I was devastated and humiliated. I never asked to visit again.

It was outrageous. Grandpa continued to hurt us in every way possible, even through his youngest son. Poor, hurt Randy. His simple, happy life, had been interrupted. What I had been through, the turmoil in my life was too much for him to handle. When I finally thought I was getting answers I could understand, life had given me yet another betrayal which I couldn't handle. I believe all my aunts and uncles took Grandpa's side, as he called me a liar over and over again. The only two who truly believed me were Mom and Uncle Landon; for they had been first hand witnesses of the rage that lay within their father.

I made a statement to the social service counselors. A physical and vaginal exam was highly recommended, and mentioned to me. I refused them. It was humiliating, and yes, I felt ashamed, like a whore he swore I was. They asked my opinion. They asked me what I wanted to happen to my grandpa. They knew my feelings towards him and my struggle to decide whether I wanted him in prison. Did I want to lock him up, and throw away the key, or did I want him to get psychiatric help? I was sick with worry my family might hate me if he went to jail. I felt a heavy weight on my shoulders as to how the rest of the family would feel if I took him from their lives. Yet the possibility of help for him never felt right. I wasn't positive help could tame the beast inside him.

A "sentence" was handed down to my grandfather. He was to serve six weeks in the VA Mental Facility. The claim was mental incompetence due to shrapnel which struck him in the head during the war. Claiming he could not recall any of the events in which I cited, he was declared mentally unfit.

He was released to his wife, my grandmother, after his sentence was carried out. I wouldn't call it a sentence. I was relieved at the time that he didn't go to jail. I didn't know then the damage he had brought down on the different children he controlled. At nine years old, I had hoped it was only me.

As time passed, some acquaintances of ours come forward to me, assuring me that I was not the only one to feel his wrath. Shocked, hurt, and sick to my stomach; I wished he had been sentenced to death row. I was not his only quest. Innocent people were hurt before me, and I had not known the horrors they deserved justice for--the justice I failed to give them. How selfish of me to think he could be helped.

It was during this time that our little basement house

SHATTERED PANE

was taken away from us. The electrical lines that ran to the washer caught fire, and destroyed the dreams of having our own A-frame home. Our small basement living quarters were flooded with water from the wash machine hose which melted, and most of what we owned was ruined. We salvaged what we could, packed our meager belongings into Mom's car, and left. We went back to the city, and rented a small house. We might never have a chance to live in a house we actually owned, but it was good that we left. It was time to get away from the knowing glances of people who knew; the pitiful looks from those who felt sorry for me. It was time to start a new, safe life – Me, Mom and Gage--just the three of us. No one else would be there. No one could hurt us.

The small two bedroom white house was nice. It had a nice yard, and was gently shaded with old Oak trees. The single car port shielded Mom's car in the nasty weather, and provided a nice covered area to play games. I was in the third grade when we moved in. The reason I remember is because our landlord was also my third grade teacher.

Social Services was at the door of our new little safe-house shortly after. They wanted to remove me from my mother's custody, and place me in a home until things were was sorted out. Mom and Grandma refused to let them take me. She convinced them that we were out of his house, and I was safe. She told them we were prosecuting, and my protection was insured.

I started school there. I had already been there for kindergarten and made a few friends. I was able to rekindle my old acquaintances. Brittney became my first close friend.

Chapter 11

Family

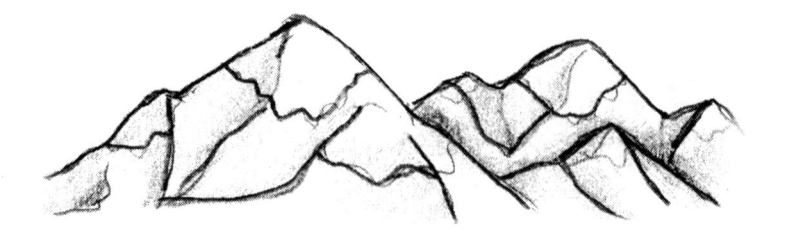

By this time my dad met a woman who became his girlfriend, Diana. She was a little shorter than my mom, with uncontrollable blond curls and thick glasses that hid her pretty blue eyes. She was nice to us and was a great cook. She and Dad tried making this point in my life happy by taking us places and doing things we couldn't do with Mom. I think he was trying to make up for his crime against me. Dad never pursued me. I wasn't fearful that he would ever bother me again although I don't know why. Maybe I just didn't feel like worrying about it anymore. So we trudged along like a normal, divorced family. My dad took a good position at Merck, and for the first time had good benefits, and vacation time. I noticed their efforts, appreciated them. At this point in my life, I believe I was too scorned and exhausted to have a chance at a happy carefree childhood.

When I told my secret, Mom tried to shoot my grandfather, and our house had caught on fire. My toys, favorite dolls, clothes, and the biggest part of my childhood was gone, including my innocence. I went to school, did my homework, chores, and went on with life as if I were fine. In the mists of this confusion, my dad remarried. I was happy for him, but had mixed emotions on what it meant for my life. I didn't understand my emotions, and never will.

I remember the wedding as if it were yesterday. They looked so happy up at the altar, repeating their vows. I wanted them to be happy, but I also wanted my family back.

Diana continued to try with us. She did the best she could with what she had. She cooked our favorite meals, played games with us, and tried to make it a happy home. She wasn't mean or scornful towards either of us. She and I had a different idea in fashion though. Dad would send us shopping for school clothes, and I never liked the ones she picked out for me. I agreed to them as I didn't want to offend her and had yet to learn to stand up for myself. For some reason, it never felt normal. My entire life was not normal.

Dad and Diana planned a vacation to Colorado for all of us. It was a wonderful experience. They rented a small log cabin in the woods, with a lot of activities to keep us entertained. The most memorable one I hold was climbing a huge rock hill not far from the cabin. We brought along nuts and bread, hoping to feed the squirrels and birds. Surprisingly enough, they came to us with no fear, and ate from the palms of our hands.

We took tours, and a road to the top of Pikes Peak. The mountain was gigantic as we climbed the steep road; the car winding in, and out of the mountain side road. Wonders of the world were seen at every turn we made. Standing still, I could feel the clouds as they formed around us. I felt as though I could reach up, and shake hands with God Himself. I thanked Him for the beauty that surrounded us that day.

At this point, I was struggling in the world. I didn't know how to live in it or how to forget my past. Psychiatrist and counselors never felt right. The possibility of sharing my nightmare with a stranger was unfathomable. I know I was probably a difficult kid, but I wasn't sure what was right or wrong. I skipped a few visits to Dads on his weekends; I just didn't want to go. I wanted my life to be normal. I needed help, but my father couldn't help me. He had also transgressed against me.

I don't remember any words ever being spoken by Dad

about the things that happened with Grandpa. Visits came and went, with no words of encouragement; no communication of the things in the past. It seemed as if it was more than he could handle. Maybe he didn't want to face the truth of what happened to his daughter, or maybe he was afraid of resurrecting the memories I had. I guess he could have been afraid that his own nasty transgression would be brought to light. I lost my virginity at the tender age of eight. I knew I was the "whore" my grandfather called me. I was a walking disaster; things never went according to plan. It was then I felt the weight of emotions and depression.

It was easier to never have a dream or hope for the future. As much as I wanted to look for the best, I only felt the evil in my heart. My life stopped. As Grandpa said, I wasn't meant to live in this world, and wasn't worthy of the air I breathed. My body and mind turned numb, and constantly held doubts about everyone around me. Who could be trusted or who would hurt me if given a chance?

My Uncle Landon and his family moved in with us due to financial issues. He and Mom both thought it would be easier if they could split the rent. Our two bedroom house was small enough as it was. Once we packed four more people in, well, to say the least, it was incredibly crowded. So my Uncle Landon, his girlfriend, and two kids stayed with us for a while.-

Gage slept in the basement, Landon and his girlfriend, Susan, slept in the living room on the floor with Trish, the oldest child of about age three. McKenzie, who was an infant at the time, was put in a playpen in my room. If she woke up at night I was instructed to take her to her mother.

Every time I would wake Susan, she refused to get up. I tried with all my might to force her to take over child care duties for her own child. McKenzie would cry loud and strong in need of a bottle. I could not leave her unattended as I was sleep deprived enough. So I became a night time mommy at the age of nine. I never mentioned this to my mom; she had enough on her plate alone. I loved those babies, as much as I would my own. I did everything I could to help with them; I had school, and was always incredibly tired. I didn't complain to anyone. Everyone was always worried about someone or something else.

My mom focused her free time on me and the disasters that invaded my thoughts. We would talk at any and all hours that were available. She had me see several different counselors, but none were as good for me as she was. She asked me different questions hoping to learn more, and we would fall asleep crying. She was the best person I had, the only one that got me through.

Mom and I took a trip to Oklahoma with one of her friends, Peyton. My memory is poor of this trip, but I do remember laughing more than I had in a long time, and feeling at ease. We went to this little old town. I had a lot on my mind, and she knew it. We laughed, ate, swam, and had a great time together. We didn't talk of anything unpleasant. My mother is the one who made my life worth living. I thank God that it was she with me in this confusion. I could not imagine sharing this time with anyone else.

At this point, I no longer wanted to go anywhere unless it was with her. My dad never did nor said anything to me about what happened in my life. He too, had turned his back on me. Although my body healed, my mind, heart, and soul were broken. As I would look at the world around me, my vision was a blur. The edges were sharp, the pieces in disarray, never to be smooth, spotless, or clean again. I was dirty and broken, discarded by those who were supposed to love me.

Times I spent with Brittney were the times I remember feeling like a kid. Brittney was short and skinny. She had knobby knees, beautiful blue eyes, and blond hair. She wore glasses that were thick and heavy. Her face was full, and pretty with a marked dimple in her chin. We would spend the night at each other's houses, talk about our dreams, and draw on each other's backs. She had a small playhouse in her yard. It was somewhere we could go and hide away from the world. Times like that gave me enough escape from my past to keep going. They made the remaining fractured pieces of my window seem stronger.

Chapter 12

Broken

It didn't take long for Landon to get on his feet, and find a place of his own, which meant Mom struggled again to make the rent. When the lease was up, she found a cheaper place on Main Street. A small two bedroom town house. The rent was low, and we had the extra bedroom to take in a tenant. Mom's friend, Kay, moved into the spare bedroom.

With Kay helping with the rent and utilities, Mom could start a savings account for the things we needed most. Mom had her king size bed and all her bedroom furniture crammed into the master bedroom. We literally had to cross the bed to get to the dresser on the other side. In its own way, it was comical, us climbing over the bed to get to our clothes. Yes, it was a tight fit, but I felt safe having them with me. Eventually, a bed was put in the basement for Gage so he could have his own space.

Mom worked twelve hour days, and overtime when it was offered. Her hours were from noon to midnight. The only time we saw her were her days off. She would always leave me a note to find in the morning when I woke up, and I would write her back about my day before bed. It was hard, but we understood that she needed to work for money to support us. It was a mentally and physically demanding job. I could see the havoc it wreaked on her body.

Then, Kay had a family emergency; her mother was ill, and needed 'round the clock care. She needed to move in with her family so she could help as much as possible. It was sad watching her leave, I had grown to care about her during her brief stay.

It seemed like everyone we knew was always shuffling, struggling, and moving around to make ends meet. Someone always needed help, or had a crisis. People always drifted in, and out of our lives. Kay drifted out, and it was just the three of us once again; just the way I liked it. Us against the world.

We were not old enough to stay on our own, and Mom worried constantly. Gage was almost twelve; I was close to ten. She enlisted the help of a neighbor in a unit a couple doors down. She was a single mother, and raised her twin seventeen year old boys alone. She understood how hard it was, and agreed to check in on us from time to time in the evening.

It was great. Gage and I were on our own. My homework was always done, and we did our best with cleaning and cooking. Gage did most of the cooking because he was scared to let me use the stove. He was constantly afraid I would hurt myself. We lived off rice, pizza, spaghetti, cereal, and macaroni & cheese. Whatever was available, and anything he could cook.

He did his best to make sure I was taken care of, but I'm sure it was a nuisance to him. He had his own things to do, and friends to hang out with. Raising his baby sister was not on his top priority list, yet he never complained. We fought as normal siblings do, but he was always right there when I needed him most.

The best days were when Mom would make a crock pot meal, or left food for us to reheat. It was a nice change. She did that as often as she could. It was well appreciated.

I saw counselors and psychiatrists because of Grandpa. Those were good days, too. Not because I enjoyed going, but because she took off work to take me. It was a combination of laughter and tears.

SHATTERED PANE

Being in that situation, and going through it, was like a knife to the heart. I wanted so badly to know what normal was like. I was a whole ten years old, and a carefree childhood was already ruined for me. Normal was way out of my grasp. I always have, and always will feel the hurt and judgment Grandpa laid on me so harshly. It stuck in my mind as though it was plastered there with crazy glue. I was his little whore, and felt as though I always would be.

The lady down the street eventually grew tired of checking on us, so she enlisted the help of her twin sons. Unfortunately, they failed to mention the arrangement with my mom. It worked fine, so there was no need to mention it; it would only cause more worry.

I can't remember when or how the duties were switched. All I know is that it was spring time, and Gage and I both loved being outside. Him with his skateboard or bike, and me with my favorite doll or skates. The twins were nice enough. They'd knock on the door, ask if we were okay, and go on about their business, hanging out with their friends. If we were outside, they would ask if we needed anything or if they could help in any way.

We had driveways and parking in the front and back that were perfect for riding our bikes or roller skating. I had a couple friends who lived in the houses on the other side of the main street. I could sit and watch them from the front step as the fathers mowed the lawns, mothers planted flowers, and the children tumbled about in the grass. They seemed so normal. Next door to our townhouse was a small row of ranch type apartments. It gave us plenty of room to play and ride bikes.

The twins and their friends quickly lost interest in trying to watch out for us as they began smoking, drinking, and using various drugs in their nightly schedule. So I stayed close to the townhouse, and didn't wander off much. I didn't like their friends at all. They were all big, cussed a lot, hung out in the parking lot, and picked on me because of my doll and stroller. I stayed in the front or inside as much as possible.

One evening, Alfred, one of the twins, saw me sitting on the front step. He came over, and sat down next to me. I was working on my homework, and he offered to help. He was seventeen. I never really knew a teenager other than my cousin Mike. Wide hard shoulders, and bulky arms framed his dirty 6' stature.

He looked over at me with his dark brown eyes as though a question turned his smile into a smirk. The boys looked the same, but I could easily tell them apart. Alfred was dirty, and high most of the time; more gruff than Joey. Joey was the same size, but his smile was sweet, and his brown eyes would glisten in the sun when he looked at me. Clean and sincere.

I tried to always be aware of who I was with. Alfred said he was taking a walk; he was tired of being a "nobody" like his friends. He seemed saddened, and hurt by his "buddies". He asked me if I wanted to walk with him, because I wasn't supposed to be alone without them or my brother. So I did. We walked towards the small apartments on the side of our building, they gave me the creeps.

He must have felt my fear, took my hand in his, and smiled. His hand was soft and comforting. I wasn't scared with him at my side. The sun was shining, and people were out working on their lawns and houses.

We passed one of the complexes when he said it was time to turn around. Instead of going back the way we came, he guided me through two of them assuring me it was just a short cut. The bushes were untrimmed, it was a tight fit between them, and the hard scratchy wall of dark brown brick.

It wasn't a short cut at all, it was a path straight back to hell. He lifted me off the ground, and slammed me up against the brick. The rough edging tore into my back as my head slammed into the hard surface. My feet dangled, I was higher, and taller than him. All I could see was his head, and the tall overgrown bushes. He told me to shut up, and dropped me to my knees. My shirt was torn, and my back was cut as I slid down the wall. He eagerly peeled away my shorts, clawing at me, and quickly had me naked from the waist down. It happened so fast I barely had time to react. I could smell the sweat, and madness into which he had evolved. The familiar fear crept into my gut, I knew what was happening. His left hand captured me by the hair, and collar of my shirt; forcing my face upwards. His right hand was forced inside of me. Once again, I felt the tear as a scream threatened to be freed. I thought this was over. That moment I knew this was my life, and it would never change.

His hard, stiff penis was forced into me. I fought hard; I grabbed at the bushes to get loose from his unyielding grip. Each whimper was welcomed with a tight squeeze at my throat. I gasped for air as his hand wrapped tighter and tighter around my throat. He was strangling me. My eyes felt like they would burst under the pressure. I thought I was dying when he released his grip. Then, in an instant he was done, he got up, and left without a word. I curled up on the ground and cried, desperately choking for air. I scrambled to get my clothes back on before anyone could see. Blood dripping down my thighs, and horrid pains in my body once again. Just as I thought my life could be good, it happened again. How many evil people could I fight off? There was no more clarity, my window was in disarray, and it became filthy, layered with a coat of smoke and haze. It was like everything, and everyone demanded my silence. I was meant to be used, to be a sexual boxing bag.

It didn't end there. There were several more forceful trips to the short cut, only he started bringing his brother, Joey, along. Alfred carried a small pair of pliers in his hand. If I made a sound or protest, he would squeeze it on the inside of my palm or my finger tip until it pinched my skin so hard it would bleed.

I couldn't wait for school to start. I was ten years old and school was my safe haven. Joey and his brother fought all the time. Joey didn't want to participate, but his brother kept a hold on him too. Alfred had a sick perversion, and was more powerful than Joey. Alfred always ended up winning. Joey felt trapped like me--speaking apologies in my ear while the rape was occurring. Most of the time they both had a turn. If it was one on one; it was always Alfred, angry and violent. If I did something wrong, he started my punishment with forcing me to inhale full unfiltered camel cigarettes, followed by a kick from his boot to my ribs as I struggled to let the smoke loose. Alfred would laugh at me, and call me a baby while I was still gasping for air. It burned as I forced it into my throat and lungs. If I refused, he left painful burns on my private areas or anywhere he deemed fit.

They started learning Gage's schedule, and eventually moved the "party" to the basement of my house. Alfred started using cocaine and heroin in his daily schedule. I had not been in counseling long enough to understand that this was not my fault. I could barely discuss the previous episodes about Grandpa, much less reveal this. I often wondered if rape and beatings occurred in every young girl's life. I couldn't image it would happen to me alone. It's possible, like me, they hid it well. Fighting the same mental and physical battles as I was.

My body became nothing but hidden bruises, and I was begging for the calming effect of nicotine by then. It became my friend, and the rush of nicotine was the only thing I could lose myself in. It became my comfort zone, a blanket I could sink into.

Joey confronted him; Alfred hit him upside the head, and kicked his legs out from under him. Alfred forced Joey to rape me as he whipped us both with a belt. Every blow would be followed by an apology in my ear from Joey. I could see the pain in his face, and eyes, as each whip of the belt hit, striking with a loud smack to his back, and searing the flesh on my side. He was on top, so he took the full force of the blows. He covered me the best he could. With each whip that occurred, he unintentionally crushed the air out of my lungs, trying to protect me from the agonizing searing sting that followed. I bit my lip to quiet my screams, and hid my face so he would not witness the tears that sprung from my eyes.

Days were a blur. On the days in between, Alfred would smile, and talk to me as if I were an old friend or confidant. Never knowing ahead of time when his bi-polar mind would switch. He was two different people. I kept my distance, and stayed inside.

Alfred taught me the technique of oral sex. I refused several times, but any rejection I made was followed by a burn, or cut on my private areas or worse. The thought made me gag. I consented reluctantly to save myself from more injuries. He was dirty, smelling of stagnant sweat and urine. The taste was salty and stale. His hand wouldn't allow me to take a breath, but pulled my head in to force it down my throat further, as my stomach threatened to vomit. The furnace moaned loudly in the background. It became my focus for the harshest realities. His release came quickly as his foul, slimy liquid discharged in my mouth, and all over my face. I gagged at the putrid smell, fell to the side, and vomited on the floor. I was left with a burn on my chin as he made me wash it up before Gage returned from his friends.

One of the burns on my backside became severely infected. It was painful, swollen and oozing puss. Joey noticed, and started treating it by draining the infection, using antibiotic cream, and bandaging it before he left. He did this as often as possible until he was confident it would heal correctly.

Alfred always carried his small, yet incredibly sharp, pocket knife. He held it to my throat when he wanted to use objects before himself. Once, I caught him with my tooth during oral sex. He grabbed my throat, and pressed a cigarette into the side of my shoulder. If I couldn't get my hips correct, or my legs wide enough, more burns or painful wounds would be made. In his anger, and frustration he used his knife to slice a slit on my vagina's outer lip; just because I scooted away from him.

SHATTERED PANE

At this point, they were getting high every day. Alfred thought it would take some of the struggle out of me, if I too, were high. I refused the first three times, only to be left with more burns on my face and vagina. So I relented, and smoked along with them. He was right. I couldn't struggle or fight as well. It left a numbing sensation in my head. I kept getting high, and started visiting my mindful place more often than not. If Alfred caught me not paying attention, he would fly off into a fit of rage. Joey was happy I found a way to tuck inside myself and hide.

Sometimes, I wasn't even sure what I did wrong, and he would hurt me again where ever he chose. I explained my visual wounds to my mom with one excuse after the after another. She knew I was trying to learn to ride the skate board, and I was always on roller skates. Sometimes Alfred scratched the burn he left, and turned it into a deep dark gash, so I could explain it away with a fall.

Alfred announced one day that we were having a surprise guest, and he wanted me to pose naked. The perfect pose in the perfect light. He was inviting a friend to a party. He held me in position, but I was not happy. He placed the knife, blade side up, to the back of my neck, and told me to look like I was enjoying myself as they both showered me with normal and gentle strokes and kisses. They treated me like a princess. I felt disgusting and dirty.

As I watched the stairs, footsteps appeared. I could not believe my eyes as Gage ascended the stairs. A loud gasp escaped my throat when I saw him. I was humiliated, embarrassed, and ashamed. They kept him on the steps while they would both take turns. I had to fake that I liked it. Alfred's knife would pull closer, so close that I could feel the sharpness of the blade on my neck, hearing the slight slices on small sections of my hair. Forcing my tears back, and a smile on my lips. I kept my eyes closed, I just couldn't look at him.

I will never forget the look on Gage's face when he left. At that moment, I became a wicked slut in his eyes. He never gave me a chance to share my side of the story. I was so ashamed I couldn't even begin to get the words out to defend myself, so I never pushed or mentioned it. How could I explain it was all an act to keep from being hurt? He saw me smile. He saw me moan. He never knew the blade in Alfred's hand was my acting coach.

In my head, I knew what was happening was wrong. I understood Gages feeling of hatred towards me. I knew then and there I was a slut, a whore, and Satan himself had me in his clutches.

I decided to tell Mom I needed her help. My prayers for help had gone unanswered, my only hope was that she could forgive me, and they wouldn't hurt us anymore. I was beaten so badly in body and spirit; I had no physical or mental strength left. I could not win this war alone.

She came home from work; Gage locked himself in the bedroom; and I told her the story. I cried as I tried to explain, but my words were never complete. I mumbled the whole sordid story to her, once again seeing the shock register on her slight features. I hated it. I hated the hurt, and disappointment I gave her. I couldn't understand why I didn't stop it, or why I didn't come to her sooner.

She called the police, and took off for the lady down the street. She called them out, but I'm sure the boys heard her coming and ran off. I shut myself down, and cannot for the life of me remember what happened next. The police knew who they were but they were never found. I guess they ran away. Good riddance. Their mother told the police she had no idea where they could have gone. She maintained their innocence; she never raised her sons to become monsters. My dad was not at my side. My dad did not show up, nor did he ever mentioned a word to me about it. It wasn't until later in life I learned he had never been told. The whole terrifying night was a blur.

I learned one of the most valuable lessons of my life that day from my Mom. I was depressed, suicidal, and just didn't care anymore. I was crying uncontrollably. My Mom pulled me to the bathroom mirror, made me look at myself, and recite these words after her: "I am smarter than I think, I am stronger than I believe, and I hold the power that will get me through anything God throws at me". Anytime I feel my life falling, I go to the mirror, and recite that to myself, over and over again until I believe it.

Chapter 13

Friendships

The next day was moving day once again. We moved out of the townhouse, and into my mom's friend's house. Her name was Peyton, and she was different, but all my mom's friends had their quirks. Peyton had short blond hair, big blue eyes, and had once worked as a Playboy Bunny in her late teens. My mom knew her from working at the factory. They were already friends. Since we needed someplace fast, we accepted her offer to move in. She taught me a lot. Posture, hygiene, and certain lessons I never knew about. I agreed with some things, such as washing your hair twice, showering every day, good posture, and highlights in my hair. However, the fact that a man always notices if your toenails and fingernails match is a whole different story. She was full of useful and trivial information. She was smart, funny, and sweet. I didn't care for the know-it-all attitude she brought forth sometimes, but it was a nice house to live in with white siding, a black door, and shutters. It was a bonus that I had my own room with a water bed, and a pool out back. It also gave my mom some time to enjoy herself, relax, and save some money. At that time in their lives, they were good for each other.

At this point, life was more normal than I had remembered. Unfortunately, my self-esteem was incredibly low, my self-confidence, and depression even worse. I didn't care whether I lived or died. Actually, I preferred that death would come quickly, in a natural way. I continued each day, going through the motions of a normal ten year old child. As hard as I would try, normal was never a part of my life.

I met two girls on our block. Sarah, Jenny, and I quickly became best friends. We walked the subdivision for hours on end. We would find a drainage platform, sit and talk for hours, sharing our hopes and dreams for the future. We held sleepovers and were constantly at the skating rink. My friends and I would go on Friday nights and Saturdays if we could. The speed of the skates beneath my strong feet, the pounding of music in my ears, and the flashing lights left me dancing on wheels all night. It was a natural high I could experience alone or with friends. It was my passion.

Gage made friends, too. His passion was to be outside riding his bike, mowing grass for money, or on his skateboard. He started drinking with Peyton's son, Jim, who lived in the basement. He was tall with long jet black hair, and ocean blue eyes. He was kind to me, but he kept his distance. Maybe he heard about my past, and didn't want to scare me. He never got too close, and that was fine with me.

The drinking started slow, but Mom came home from work early one day only to find Gage completely drunk and vomiting in the toilet. There was no one there on a constant basis to watch over us. Mom and Peyton both worked the swing shift so there was never a set schedule as to when one or the other would be home. So, my parents decided it would be best if Gage went to live with our dad.

My mom and Peyton started getting into astrology. After that it was psychics and the Ouija board. I found the psychics both amusing, and intriguing. One of them told my mother, that I would run away, but that she would find me on the second night and fix the issues at hand. It was a ridiculous thought. I didn't want to leave.

They had their nights were they could go out and cut loose; sometimes I would go, and sometimes I would stay home. I was completely comfortable with Jim. I was just another person in his house, and he didn't pay much attention to me or my activities.

The time I spent with my friends was fun. Kids my age were drama queens, but for the most part we didn't do much but laugh. I found some freedom, didn't have to look over my shoulder, and wait for predators to overtake me. My friends were with me, and there was always safety in numbers.

In the absence of abuse, in the presence of counseling from Mom and a licensed counselor, I began to feel a little stronger, both mentally and physically. My mom helped me fight for my confidence and was my rock getting me through each day. Things weren't perfect, but they were a far cry from the terror I had once lived. The large pieces of my shattered window pane were clearing.

I learned quickly that as painful as it might be, talking and sharing made a huge impact on how to live with my horrors. My mom was never critical, even in the worst of situations. She knew how I felt more than anyone ever could. She suffered the same as I did, but I believe that her talking with me, helped her to recover a bit as well. Of course, Mom also took me to a counselor. She knew I needed more help than she alone could give me.

Chapter 14

Angel

Dad and Diana moved into a quaint new house. The front was covered with a dark red brick with a long driveway. My dad put in a tire swing, and a basketball hoop to help occupy our time. I guess I was happy for him, and his new wife, but I felt bad for my mom who was alone, constantly struggling in one way or another.

Soon after, Diana became pregnant. Nine months later, my precious baby sister was born. It was truly one of the highlights of my life! She was the most beautiful baby I ever saw. I was eleven when she arrived. Dad took me out of school so I could meet her. It was an instant and unconditional love I had for this innocent little life. Her precious pink cheeks and the tiny squeaks filled me with a joy that was wondrous. Angel was her name, and that's exactly what she was, a beautiful angel.

She gave me something positive to talk about with the counselors. The sessions were hard to get through so sometimes I just talked a lot about her. I blocked the worst times out of my head. A counselor was helping me bring them to the surface a little at a time; we would work on one horrific truth at a time. The doctors started me on anti-depressants, anti-anxiety medicine, and constantly changed them as my depression worsened.

Counseling was a slow process. Somewhere along the way, I lost the memory of my unusual experiences with Dad. I guess time buried the memories somewhere deep in my mind: I couldn't draw the truth out. I blocked out the abuse, but pictures of him still flashed through my head. I didn't understand why I had the creepy visions, and the dreams were so clear in my mind. I went to Mom a third time to share my story, but I told her I wasn't sure, and that I knew it was crazy. I could describe the images in my head in full detail, but it all intertwined with Grandpa. Faces switched, and times ran together. The confusion was nerve racking.

My mom was incredibly calm and still, as she heard me out. It seemed almost impossible. My dad knew how difficult my mom's abuse had been on her. He even institutionalized her for it. It was hard for me to believe he would chance the same fate as hers with me. She agreed that we would not jump to conclusions, but we needed to know the truth.

We agreed that I would write him a note sharing my memories. I was afraid to outright ask him. It was the most difficult note I have ever had to write. Fear, shame, and guilt were all I felt.

By this time I had an infant baby sister, and it worried me a lot that she would fall victim to the same things I experienced, if my images were true. I needed to know if I was right, or if my mind was so scarred by men that I drifted in and out of reality. I desperately needed to find out. I had to make sure she was protected, and I was the only one who could do it. I refused to leave this sweet innocent baby's safety to chance. I needed to protect her in any way possible.

I wrote the note, made it plain and simple. Without going into detail I basically asked him if he molested me during that time. I was terrified for the outcome either way. If he was innocent, then why was I being haunted? If he was guilty, I wasn't sure if I could go on. My life was like a nightmare of horrible memories. Things would pop behind my eyes from nowhere.

I dissected every aspect of each outcome I could think

SHATTERED PANE

of. If he denied it, I would have to dig through my memories further to make sense of them. If he was guilty, and I turned him in, he could go to jail. If that happened, Angel would grow up without a father, and most likely, I would never see her again. She would always know that I took her dad away. I found it incredibly hard to live life knowing she may blame me, forever hate me. If I took my chances, made a deal with him, she could be a part of my life, and I would do anything in my power to make sure she had a chance at a good life. It didn't occur to me that I was still a child myself. At twelve, I came up with a plan to save my sister.-

I decided that if he admitted it to me, I would not go to the police. I would make him promise that he would never touch or hurt Angel; that he would treat her like a princess, and would never turn his back on her or any other child he produced.

Mom and I drove to his house, and gave him my note. I waited in the car for Mom to wave me in. To my surprise, he admitted it; he shared his side of the story with my mom and Diana. His recollection of the abuse did not match mine. He explained that we were sleeping, he rolled over, felt me beside him, and one thing led to another. Just one lonely night. I didn't remember the night his story was about, but I made a deal with the devil. I would not turn him over to the police if he promised to make Angel the center of his world, and to never touch or harm her in anyway. I would be watching, and checking. If she indicated in any way, any foul play, I would turn him in, and tell my side of the story. We had his confession on tape. He couldn't run from that.

In return, I was never to let Angel know anything about

it. I felt forced to leave it in the hands of God and Dad. I learned from an early age that the people I loved the most were usually the ones I couldn't trust, and hurt me the most. The only exception that ever stayed true was my mom, but I would be different. I would never hurt Angel, and I would keep her safe. I was an expert on sexual abuse, and I would always be on the lookout for signs of it in her. Diana became stressed and irritable. I don't think she wanted me in their lives after she learned about dad. I was never sure if she hated me because it happened, or loathed me for asking for the truth.

One day, on a weekend I was visiting my dad, I played with Angel the whole time. She was a bright, happy, and smart toddler. When it was time for me to go home, she cried for me at the door; begging for me to come back. I got in the car, and started to cry. My dad sent me back in to give her one last hug. He knew it hurt me to see her that way. So I went back in and picked her up. I hugged and kissed her as much as I could. I never wanted to let her go. I would drown myself in her smell, smile, and her innocence was locked in my heart forever.

Diana came in from the kitchen, and yanked her harshly from my arms. She shoved me out the door. It slammed hard behind me. I got in the car, with a sting in my eyes, and a hurt in my heart so strong, I literally felt like a witch. My dad asked me about it before leaving the driveway, and went back in the house for a few minutes.

That night my dad called my mom, and told her that Diana left him. She returned a couple days later to try to make things work. The situation was hard in every way possible. The stress took over. It wasn't long before my dad put her into a mental institution for a nervous breakdown, just like he did my mom.

I continued therapy and tried to work through the stupid things that happened. I was already hooked on cigarettes and marijuana from Joey and Alfred, and I had no want or will to live. I started experimenting with anything I could find, in hopes that something would take away the monsters that haunted me at night. I knew in my heart it would be easier on everyone around me if I would just walk away. I wouldn't be able to hurt anyone ever again. My mother who suffered so much because of me, my brother who couldn't stand me after he witnessed my act with the twins, and my family who was divided all because of what happened to me…me.

One day when I came home from an especially bad day at school, my mom, my grandma, and my grandfather were waiting for me at the house. I almost vomited when I saw him there, sitting on the couch, in my home. The familiar smell and fear crept into me. My body trembled, panic swelled, and I couldn't speak. He defiled my safe house just by being in it. I was already down and depressed. Then I walked in to find *him* there. Grandma brought him over so he could apologize, as though that would make everything all right. I couldn't accept his apology, not at that point. They said what they needed to and left.

I felt as though I couldn't handle any more and had a breakdown right there. Crying my eyes out. I told Mom that I just wanted to run away. I couldn't find another way out. She said yes. I asked yes to what. She said, let's just pack our suitcases, and run away for a little bit. So that is what we did.

JENNA K. SCOTT

We packed for the weekend, drove away, and ended up in a paradise hotel in the city. Away from everyone. It was liberating. We stayed there for the weekend. We ate nice dinners, swam in the indoor pool, talked about anything except our problems, and watched TV. It was just what the doctor ordered.

Chapter 15

Urgent

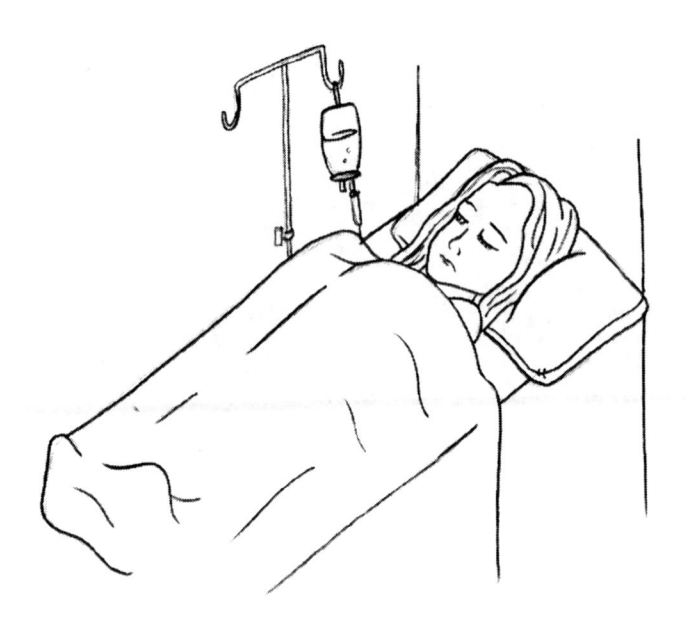

E very day I went to school, I watched as bullies picked on, teased, or hurt my friends in any way possible. Everyone was convinced that my mom was a witch, if they messed with me, she could easily cast a spell on them, or work up a voodoo doll in their name. I was never harassed.

One day, I was walking through the halls at school, going to my next class. I saw Brittney in her cheerleading uniform backed into the lockers, surrounded by other girls, and a lot of giant guys. One was talking to her; he didn't look happy. All I could see was the expression on her face, and her body language. She was my friend, and she was scared. That was all it took. I couldn't hear the conversation, but I knew it wasn't nice. Brittney's body was stopped by the locker, her head face upwards, her eyes were huge, and her face fearful. I squeezed through the crowd, pulled her out of there fast, and we walked to class together.

I never did know exactly what he said, but it didn't matter. I never forgot the hurtful look in her eyes, and had an intense drive to protect my friend. The guy who was talking down to her rode my bus. I didn't know his name, but I knew where he lived. That afternoon, I did not get off at my stop. I got off at his.

I confronted him without fear. He pushed me away. The more I hollered the more he pushed. He didn't scare me. I may not have been able to protect myself from harm before, but I discovered I had a strength, and a fierce protective instinct when someone tried to hurt a person I cared about. With one quick grab of his arm, a swift kick to buckle his knees, he was on the ground. With a tenacity that surprised us both, I threatened him to go nowhere near her ever again. I stormed off and headed home. My anger subsided, my stride metamorphasized into something darn near a skip, and I made it home with a grin on my face.

Watching anyone bully the people I knew (and even the ones I didn't) made me incredibly furious. A notorious school bully wanted to fight it out between her and me after school. I was ready. I was going to teach her a quick lesson. We met, we fought, and I won. It didn't take long before I was also fighting guys. With the exception of a few times, I won.

It became a regular routine for me to stand up to bullies. I faced down much bigger, scarier monsters than these jerks, and made it out alive. I overcame living with true life beasts; there wasn't a bully in the school who could scare me. It was as if I became invincible. I didn't care how big my opponent was. I found a new passion. I became the bully's bully.

I started to come to school prepared. I learned quickly the pain little things could give. So I always made sure I had my bag of tricks with me. Sharp rings on each finger, bracelets with spikes, and a sliver of a razor blade embedded in my boots. I was on the lookout for anyone who bullied someone continuously. A plan was necessary; I could look at them and know their weak spots. I always arranged it in my mind; I would meet them at their bus stop after school. The majority of the time, they wouldn't get off the bus. This became my way of fighting for the victims. The victim I once was.

I continued my fights. I didn't care if I was hurt or not. I'd gotten used to pain, and knew how to prepare myself for it. I was always high on one drug or another, so the pain was usually numbed anyway. When I was using, I felt like there was more power behind my blows. Every time I came out on top, I felt like a winner. I maintained my stance against injustice. I only intervened when it was a case of a bully versus an innocent.

Sometime during my 7th grade year I started having severe stomach pains. My doctor discovered a mass covering my appendix, but couldn't get clear enough images to determine the source. I was admitted, and underwent exploratory surgery to remove whatever it was inside. It turned out that my bowels somehow twisted around my appendix, and ran the risk of rupturing. They untangled my intestines, and removed my appendix.

When I opened my eyes the first time, I saw my mom and dad at the foot of the bed. Standing there together waiting for me to wake from the anesthetic. My sight was blurred, and in my drug induced state, it was almost as if it were a dream. What I saw, was heaven on earth. My mom was worried, and my dad comforted her. I dozed in and out, but I will never forget that one fuzzy moment. For just a second, it took me back to the foundation of love in which I was conceived.

While recuperating at home, I was able to spend extra time with Mom. She took off work to care for me. I shared my dreams of her of having our own house. I knew it wasn't possible, but it was something I desperately longed for. It would be she and I against the world. I didn't know it then, but my mom decided at that moment to move heaven and earth to make it happen.

My friend, Jenny, and her family moved due to her dad's job transfer. I was unaware, but my mom put a contract down on their house. They accepted the bid, and we moved in quickly. I was shocked, amazed, and overcome with a heartfelt happiness I never felt before. I knew she did it for me - our own place, my dream, came true.

    The house was a small ranch, with everything we needed, and more. It was cozy and warm. Every room held a sense of comfort and serenity. We played games on Moms nights off, I finally really felt safe. It was more than I had ever hoped for us. Like a fairytale house that princesses lived in. This one was ours. It created warm fuzzy feelings in my stomach as I would curl up in bed with a good book or homework.

    I came home from my friends one evening to find Gage visiting, and my mom having a couple of drinks. She was a little tipsy when she mentioned to Gage how much she disliked the wall petition between the kitchen and dining area. Gage brought his friend with him that night, so right then and there he started taking the wall down with a sledge hammer. Full cabinets, and a pantry of food came down in chunks. He didn't even take the time to empty any of it. My mom was thrilled as she watched him in Hulk mode. I think it gave Gage a sense of satisfaction to do this for our mother…plus it was fun! His middle name should have been destruction. It was the best way for him to let out all his anger out, get something accomplished, and pour all his strength into each blow.

    I emptied the pantry, and cabinets as they hammered away. I hopped out with armfuls of pantry items in between swings. Mom deserved a chance to just sit and be happy. There was nothing I loved more than to see a smile on her beautiful face. It was a good day. We laughed so hard at the comical antics the boys were making as they swung sledge hammers to a tune.

Chapter 16

Enemies Bond

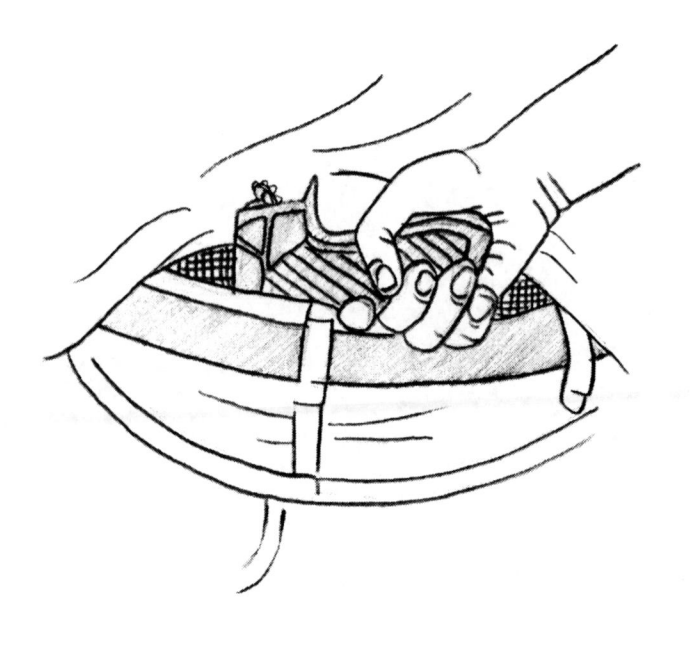

At this point, my mom discovered she had an older sister; I had another aunt. Apparently, my grandfather was married before my grandmother came into his life and had a daughter. She was an infant when he left, never to be heard from again. Nobody in the family knew they existed. It was odd, yet intriguing, to meet a new member of the family.

Her name was Dina, she was married to a man named Roy. I also had three new cousins. We went to meet them for the first time. Aunt Dina was tall, a little overweight, with wonderful blue eyes, and brown wavy hair. Uncle Roy was shorter than his wife; heavier with light brown hair and a smile hidden in his full face. Their kids were older than me. When we visited, I wandered around the property or sat and admired the massive collection of dolls Dina collected.

We got to know each other well, and eventually the conversation turned to Grandpa and me. Dina had her own story to tell. Unfortunately, he hurt them as well. He left, taking all the money they owned. Leaving his wife to support their child on her own. Never to see or find him again. She grew up in poverty, never knowing any luxuries in life. Struggling constantly to make ends meet. He left a hole in her heart where a father should have been.

I was incredibly sad to have had the opportunity to send him to jail, and to have let it slip through my little fingers; only to find out how many more people he hurt. I let my fear stand in the way of that when I talked to Child Services that day. It felt as though I held the power to decide his fate, otherwise, why would they have asked me what I wanted to happen to him. Several times I have wanted to kick myself for not asking for a more severe punishment.

We were in our little Gray house a short time before the bills started piling up. Mom started robbing Peter to pay Paul. Utilities were shut off, one after the other. We weren't the only ones in trouble.

My Aunt Sara was in serious trouble. My uncle Jude was beating her, and the girls. He whipped little Chloe with an extension cord all down her back and legs, for not eating her peas. Sara called my Grandma; she was going to leave after Jude went to work for the night. My Uncle Randy, Grandma, and Grandpa, picked them up, and took them to safety. They ended up at a women's shelter two hours away. We drove up a few times to visit, and take them things they needed.

Aunt Sara needed our help. She needed someplace for her and the girls to live until she got on her feet. It didn't take long before we added three more bedrooms in the basement. They moved in once the court issued restraining order against Jude went into effect. So our house of two, became a house of six. We were a little crowded again, but I didn't mind at all. I loved Aunt Sara, and all three of her girls.

My mom and Sara both worked second shift. I took on the responsibility of looking after Jade, Chloe and McKenna. All three of them were different in appearances, and personalities. Jade, was eleven, Chloe, seven, and McKenna, just three years old. They were great kids. They were smart, lively, and a joy to have around.

Sarah's ex-husband Jude had a smaller build for a man. He slouched, showing no hint of muscle tone in his petite frame. His face was drawn in and thin, with a stubbly beard. His hair dark brown, dirty, and shaggy. With his sad brown

SHATTERED PANE

eyes, and disheveled clothing; he appeared to not have bathed in quite some time.

He was not allowed to see his kids without court supervision. It didn't stop him from calling or showing up at the house when our Moms were at work. He scared me numerous times, calling with various threats of taking his girls, no matter what the cost.

Jude came to the house one day unannounced; just showed up out of nowhere. My mom, and Sara were both at work. The girls saw him before I could get to him, and ran to greet their daddy. McKenna was an inquisitive toddler. She climbed into the back seat of Jude's small white car, and came out holding a gun. When he saw her with it, he swiftly grabbed it, and tucked it in his pants. That instantly got me on the phone with my friend Jared explaining what was going on.

Jared was older, strong and tough. He grabbed some of his friends, and they all came down the street looking like a mob. Jude didn't know them, but the girls and I did. Jared picked Chloe up, and wrapped her in a big bear hug. Before I knew what was happening, Jared and his friends had Jude and the girls in the back yard playing whiffle ball.

My mom, and Sara arrived as quickly as they could. The game dispersed, most of the guys left, and we pulled the girls inside. Aunt Sara was in the front yelling at Jude with my mom at her side. She allowed him to say good bye to the girls, when she was sure the gun was put away. Then, she quickly ushered everyone back in the house.

Jude didn't come around much after that, and when he did, he behaved himself. He knew Sara had Mom, Jared, and his buddies, and me to stand up for her justice now. Jude, being the bully he was, backed down as bullies usually do when they're confronted. Mom and I...fighting off the bad guys. Yeah! Sara and the girls were doing well. She acquired a good stable job, a nice boyfriend, and money in the bank. They were able to move out on their own, and into a nice condo.

Chapter 17

Fate

As usual, it didn't take long before someone else was in need of a home. There was always someone in need, and Mom always took them in. Her heart was big enough to care for any needy person that came along. Sometimes it worked out, and other times it didn't. So Mom's friend Betsy, and her daughter, Corrine, moved in with us. Betsy helped with the bills, and Corrine kept me company. She was only a year younger than me. She was petite, quiet, and shy to strangers. We became more like sisters at the time, than just friends hanging out.

Little did we know that Corrine and I would be a bad influence each other. We partied together and skipped school just to hang out. We got caught and grounded a couple of times, but it didn't stop us. We snuck out nightly and partied at our friend's house. We got along great. It was incredibly fun-- drinking, drugging, and partying until late in the night.

I went to a party one night, and was talking to my friend Evan. I was trying to keep him from a fight he would never win. Evan carried a small build for someone his age. His green eyes gazed at me in a drug fueled rage. He also suffered serious brain trauma from an accident he was in years before, and could be mentally unstable. The fight was between him and Jared. It didn't take a genius to know who would win.

His girlfriend became jealous because we were talking, and decided she would put me in my place. She grabbed me by the back of the hair, and ripped a special necklace from my throat in the process. My mom had just given it to me as a gift of courage and accomplishment. I was furious! The only people who ever grabbed my hair like that were the vile monsters who hurt me so badly. As I felt her fingers grasp onto my hair, I flashed back and was filled instantly with a rage I never felt as a child. I wanted revenge, and I was about to get it. She had no idea the demons she released when she took hold of me. Fire and fury burned from the inside out. I jumped quickly to my feet and regained my balance. She started swinging. I stood by a rule to never be the first to throw a punch. I never went against that rule.

She swung and missed...swung and missed. I dodged her swings, until one made contact. Ducking and dodging. I swung back; and landed an excellent blow to her chin. I think that was the hardest I ever hit anyone in my life. Her jaw took the brunt of my fist. She managed to get up and came at me once again; at the last minute; I turned sideways, and she fell, landing hard in the grass. Once again, she charged at me. As she passed, I grabbed her hair, shoved her head hard in a flash, and she hit the concrete. She didn't get back up.

I went in search for my necklace. It laid in the grass and sparkled under the moonlight of the night. I found Corrine, and we left. I never looked back to see if the girl was okay. The following day at school, the news traveled fast. I found out she was taken to the hospital the night before by ambulance. Her diagnosis, was a fractured skull. I fractured another person's *skull* because she grabbed my hair. Her prognosis was good, but all I could think about was what could have happened. I was completely out of control and didn't care what happened to her for that one venomous moment. It scared the hell out of me that I could have killed that girl, and all I felt was my own seething anger. I never wanted to get that mad and lose control like that again. I never fought

SHATTERED PANE

again. Honestly, I never had to. My reputation was set in stone, and no one dared to mess with me.

Corrine and I decided to skip school once again. It wasn't until afterwards that we remembered both our mothers claimed if it happened again we would be moving in with our fathers. At the time, they were adamant it would happen. That was a thought I couldn't handle, and neither could Corrine. Her life was about as messed up as mine. So, in a drugged induced state, we decided to make it on our own. As cliché has it, at fifteen, we knew everything.

I knew it would be best for everyone I loved if I was gone, not ruining their lives any more. So we ran. The first night my friend Olivia, unlocked her dad's office so we would have a safe place to sleep. It was comfortable and familiar to me because I worked there in my spare time.

Two days later, my mom found us at Olivia's boyfriend's brother's house in the middle of a packed party. Just like the psychic predicted. We were drinking, and using various drugs available to us that night. Mom showed up at the house, but they wouldn't let her in. She fought her way in, got past by the two huge guys at the door. She found us in a back room drunk and in an incredibly high state of mind. Yes, we were in serious trouble.

My mom already called the police to find us, and when we arrived at my house, there were police everywhere, going through our stuff in our rooms, looking for any evidence that would lead them to us. They called off the search but we were nowhere near off the hook.

One police officer approached me with a baggie in his hands. I thought for sure they found my collection of joints, and other drugs I stashed. The officer asked in a matter of fact way, "What do you think this is?" He showed me a baggie, and its contents. I couldn't contain myself as I double over, laughing so hard it brought tears to my eyes. Of course, this made them all incredibly mad. My display of outright defiance. They jumped on me hard, but I still couldn't stop laughing. When Corrine saw the package, she laughed with me.

As soon as I could calm myself, I explained to him that I had two box turtles in the basement, and it was a baggie of turtle food. The officer turned to his partner, his partner had a wide eyed expression on his face, and said "and you tasted that!" It contained dried leaves, bugs, and small worms. As disrespectful as it was, Corrine and I burst into laughter once again. They finished their paperwork. Since we were found safe, they left.

Unfortunately, that was not the end for either of our mothers. My mom was on the phone with my dad in a heated argument as to whether or not he was coming with her or not. I wasn't sure what they were talking about, but I think she threatened him within an inch of his life to get there NOW. By that time, Betsy put Corrine in the car, and they left. I didn't know where they were going and didn't find out until later. My partner in crime was gone. I was alone, drunk, and higher than a kite.

My dad arrived, and at that time I had little to say to him. He wasn't a part of my life other than birthday cards and Christmas. It was hard seeing him, knowing what happened. Every time I was with them, I would question Angel as subtly as possible about the way Dad was with her. I was always asking and watching for any sign of something gone wrong.

Dad showed up, they put me in the car, and we left. Little did I know they were admitting me to a psychiatric facility. I didn't know why it was so important to Mom that Dad was there for this. It's not like he had been there for us in a long time.

It had been hard watching him become a father to his other kid, and accept a great job. He did it all with his new family; forgetting his old one still existed. Angel was showered with toys and activities, while Mom struggled to pay the rent, buy food to feed us, and keep the utilities on. When we did get gifts from Dad and Diana, they were small and thoughtless, like a shirt or two that I would never have worn in a million years.

Later the gifts came in the form of a check. $25 every time, the reason made no difference. It was a staple for all occasions. I always knew what to expect, and it was nothing to get excited about.

I spent the next eight weeks in the psych ward, isolated from my family except during visiting hours. Test after test revealed suicidal tendencies, horrible depression, and Post Traumatic Stress Disorder. My mother came to the conclusion that my father mastered the art of inducing psychiatric disorders--not only did he screw her up enough to have her committed, but he also managed it with Diana and with me. I believe I would have been there anyway, even if Dad wasn't involved. Although he did visit, his lack of previous parenting and support cancelled out any effort he might have made to help.

The unit I was admitted to was exclusively for kids my age. We entered through two glass, locked doors. In between the doors there was a place that held a bathroom and lockers. It was there that they searched my purse, clothing, and shoes. I stood there with my long blond hair pulled back in a ponytail, a black concert t-shirt, jeans and my socks. They kept my leather jacket and tennis shoes. I was handed a cup and sent to the restroom for a sample of my urine.

As we entered the next locked door, the nurses were in an enclosed windowed room on the left. I could see the small sliding window they used for passing out medicines and various toiletries patients needed.

I was taken to a small dark room off to the left which held nothing but a bed, tightly bolted to the floor. The walls, ceiling, and floors were all plain smooth concrete. I was given a light small blanket and a disposable pillow to sleep with. Both were thin and the room was suicide proof. It was time for my parents to say goodbye. I wasn't ready to shed a tear; I couldn't. I was shocked, and terrified over the situation at hand.

Sleep didn't come that night. Shortly after my parents abandoned me in that cold drab prison, the tears came; hot, and bitter. I spent the night crying and pacing the floor. I was still high from an acid induced speed I dropped earlier that night. I paced, and I cried, wondering what it was I had gotten myself into. How long would they leave me here? Were they coming back to get me? Would I have to live here? Where were my clothes? I knew things would never be right again. I was in need of a joint and a smoke. I was scared, lonely, and a wreck.

My first morning on the floor was horrible. I was hung over, my clothes were a disaster, and I didn't know a soul. I

SHATTERED PANE

smoked cigarette after cigarette, trying anything to calm my nerves. My stomach felt sick, so I refused breakfast.

The main room was located past the nurse's station. It was enormous and wide open. Two couches sat in the middle of the room along with a pool table, television, games on shelves, and tons of books to read. It had the standard white drop ceiling, the walls were tan on top. There was a chair rail in the middle used as a divider for the dark, brick red on bottom. The colors they chose were to make it a warm, calming environment, but left me feeling exposed, and vulnerable.

The carpet seemed as though it was dyed the exact rich, dark red as the wall was painted. They quickly informed me that the windows were bullet proof. The only thing I could see through them, was the brightness of the morning. It smelled like a hospital, the lack of a welcoming aroma set the tone. I wished the window to my soul was also bullet proof, but as it stood, it was severely cracked, and clinging to the frame. Nothing could be seen through it, just mazes of fuzzy colors, streaks of tiny slithers of glass, blood stains as I tried desperately to hold it intact.

On the opposite wall from the main door, I could see the long hallway which I assumed housed the bedrooms. I wasn't allowed a tour just yet. First I was introduced to some of the patients on the floor, but I wasn't interested in making friends. The rules of the floor were shared with me by Brad and Mark, Psychiatric Technicians who ran the floor.

Mark was tall with a rounded face, and hazel eyes. His skin was smooth, and held a genuine smile. He wasn't ugly but I wouldn't call him good looking either. If his appearance lacked in any way, his personality more than made up for it.

He was incredibly sweet and made sure I understood what he was saying, whether I acknowledged him or not.

Brad had a darker skin tone, evenly chiseled features, and a head full of rich, black hair. He was more physical and loved the gym. He incorporated workouts into his therapy with patients. He taught us that some frustrations could be shed right through your pores if you sweat hard enough.

Both psych techs directed me to a conference room. My psychiatrist was sitting at the table, awaiting my arrival. I was instructed to sit in the seat directly across from him. I never did catch his name; didn't care either.

He tossed a work packet across the desk to me, asked me to read it, and answer the questions to the best of my knowledge. It was difficult, it was mainly about feelings, and how someone would handle various situations. Questions were repeated, wrote differently; looking to see if I was consistent or not, but I was not allowed to look back. Feelings, matters of the heart, and reality were not on my list of favorite topics. I spent so much time shutting down my emotions for so many years that when I was asked to express them, my mind just shut down instantly. It was hard choosing the correct words for the things I felt.

Black shapes on cardboard were next on the agenda. They all looked like paint splatter as I was asked to put a word with each one. Splatter was the definition I tried for all of them, but it wasn't what he wanted. So we did it again, and again until I found a suitable noun, verb or adjective that satisfied him. It took hours before we were done. We stopped in time for lunch, but yet again, I couldn't eat. My stomach still wasn't ready for food.

Eventually, I met my roommate. Her name was Eve. She was my size with stiff stance and a smug smile on her face. She had some winners in her family, too. Her story stemmed from a family monster who got her hooked on crack at the young age of nine.

Our room consisted of plain tan walls, a shatter proof window, small desk, dresser, and two twin size beds; one on each side of the window. We had our own bathroom and shower, but we were not allowed to have razors, hair dryers, or curling irons. Make-up was also against the rules.

Eve and I would stay awake all night and just talk. It only took a day or two to realize we could talk to the rooms on both sides of us through the air vents in the walls. Before we knew it, our conversation of two became a chat session of six. It quickly escalated down the hall. There were midnight chat sessions constantly, and it was liberating. It felt good to get one over on the staff who otherwise ruled us like little prisoners.

I became fast friends with a boy on the unit. His name was Chad. He was average height, but incredibly thin and pale. His blond hair was neatly trimmed, and he had an average sort of look about him. Except his eyes; those eyes caught your attention. There was a wounded sadness in them, and even more striking was the color of them. They were green with hints of a sapphire blue embedded in them.

His father was in prison, and his mother was addicted to drugs. His grandparents were unable to care for him, so he was placed in several different foster homes and institutions throughout his life. He had been constantly beaten and raped by both females and males. Tortured and bullied by the other kids around him. He was sweet and spoke with a quiet tone. Once in a while a flash of strength, and anger escaped his otherwise controlled demeanor. I loved those times. His will, strength, and power would show through. It thrilled me to witness his anger released. It taught me that I, too, held that power. We swapped war stories, and even though I went through my own hell, I truly felt sorry for him. It was hard to believe anyone could hurt someone as precious as him. He was a great friend and confidant.

I made friends with other troubled teens from all different walks of life. Most of their experiences were as bad as mine, if not worse. My desire for justice welled up in me with every story that was shared. Some had traveled a long way in their healing process; some couldn't speak of the horrors they endured. I couldn't fight their bullies physically of course, but I felt compelled to help them fight their inner demons.

When I felt something in the counseling sessions work for me, but not another kid, I sought them out, and tried to get them to open up. It was easier for me to focus on their issues than to relive my own nightmares. I had a knack for getting the tight-lipped kids to talk. The backgrounds a few of them shared with me were things they never discussed with the psych techs or in our group discussions. It worked with a few of them.

Just by telling their story once to me, we were able to establish a trust that could not be broken. It was me they came to when they couldn't handle it or didn't know what to do. If it was possible, and they were willing, I referred them to Mark or Brad. Sometimes they were only confident enough if I was by their side. I was helping, so the psych

SHATTERED PANE

techs allowed this to continue. The psych techs worked with me one on one to help get me through. Not only was I fighting my demons, but I was helping them fight theirs as well.

There was this one girl; her name was Jaime. She was small, petite with long beautiful strawberry blond hair. Her pale skin dotted with freckles, masked the pain she hid. Jaime completely closed herself off to the outside world. She just seemed to "exist". She went through the motions of life. I saw more hopelessness in her eyes than I had ever seen in my life. She never spoke a word in our group sessions. Or otherwise. She was there when I was admitted, and I never saw her engage in anything. The psychiatrists and techs were unable to break through to her.

During one of our sessions, something was said that struck a nerve in her. I can't recall the topic of our discussion. All my attention was focused on Jamie's face. Her body and mind started to splinter. Something not only reached her, it shattered her inner core. We tried our best to get her to open up, and share her story, even a simple word could start the healing process. Then she cracked. She screamed, and sobbed as she bolted from the room. Out of instinct, a gut reaction, I ran after her, and followed her into her room. There was a strict policy against being in another patient's room, but I didn't care. Jaime needed help, and I was at least going to try.

Brad and Mark, tried to stop me. It was too late, I was already by her side, comforting her, holding her until her body stopped its uncontrollable trembling. I whispered words of encouragement in her ear, and coached her breathing. Deep breaths in through the nose, and out through the mouth. Slowly and easily, she followed my lead.

Brad and Mark were at the door, listening to every word we spoke; ready to intervene if necessary. There was never a conscious thought, just reaction. I couldn't stop the pull that made me follow her.

After she calmed down, she looked me in the eyes, and stared at me for a while. Her sad brown eyes searching for something I will never understand. I stayed silent, giving her the time she needed to decide. When she started to talk, her voice was soft and shaky...not more than a whisper. Each sound took physical effort, as if she was a baby just learning to speak. She only managed one slow word at a time, until she gained a little bit of her confidence back.

I was afraid to hear what happened to her. I prepared myself for whatever came. Jaime and her younger sister, Jessica, had not seen nor heard from their father since her baby sister was born. Jamie had no memory of him. He called one day out of the blue, and asked their mother if he could meet them, just once, so he could see them, talk to them, and know they were okay. The girls were old enough to ask questions about their father, and Jamie's mother thought it was time they should meet. He might have an explanation as to why he left. She was hopeful it could be a step in the right direction. She was also fearful it would be a disaster in the making.

They decided a park was a safe, neutral place to meet. There were only a few people present when they pulled in. There were trees scattered throughout creating a pretty setting. Sunlight, a soft breeze, and the excitement of two little girls filled the air. The girls' eyes were fixed on the park entrance, watching for their father to arrive. Jamie could tell her mother was anxious, but she and her sister were too overwhelmed with excitement to pay much attention. They were about to meet their father for the first time in their lives.

Her father's approach was silent. He snuck up to the bench from behind. They never heard so much as a twig crack. He called out their names easily, as though he done it every day of his life…as if he were calling them in for dinner. They all turned to look at him, not knowing what to expect.

He pulled a gun from his back pocket, and rapidly shot all three of them without ever speaking another word. He then turned the gun on himself, and ended his own life. "He shot us. He just shot us all", Jamie sobbed. I wrapped her in my arms, and held her while she finally released tears of anguish, pain, and horror she kept locked up inside for two years.

Jamie was the only survivor. There was tremendous damage done to her body from the bullet. She spent months in the hospital, and then returned for retrieval of bullet fragments which the doctors missed. Jaime had not spoken a word since the incident. That day, two years later, her silence was broken.

When she couldn't cry anymore, she started asking me questions, as if I held the answers that would give her peace. As her questions poured from her lips, I did my best to have an honest answer. Some questions had no answer, or at least none I could think of; others I explained the best I could. Mark and Brad were at the door, witnessing the whole heart-wrenching mess. They dared not intrude for fear Jamie would shut down once again. Instead they stayed in the doorway, coaxing me on. I knew the more she got out the better it would be for her.

I was learning through my own counseling the healing, the impact that sharing, could have. She had two years of conversation to pour out as we sat in her room for hours that day, until her tiny form slumped over from sheer exhaustion, and she fell asleep. I pushed her hair back off her face, covered her, and watched her sleep for a moment. Then quietly made my way back to my room, climbed into bed and wept.

It wasn't long before she began sharing with the group, little pieces at a time. I stood beside her, gave her the praise, and encouragement as she needed it. The other kids noticed her progress, and were amazed at the person she became. Warm, sweet and funny. Soon others started to confide in me as well. There was a total of eighteen troubled teens on our floor, and before it was over, I sat in on the individual sessions with eleven of them, in order to help them gain trust in Mark and Brad.

I heard story after story of their heartbreak and terrifying ordeals. Each kid on that psych ward had a damn good reason to be there. Most of us worked hard to get better; to overcome the mistrust, hurt, and the betrayals our personal demons left in their wake of destruction. There were some who either couldn't, or didn't care to make any effort, and kept to themselves. The webs they cocooned themselves in were impenetrable. Most of them just sat stone-faced with a hard look in their eyes, or had already made enough progress on their own.

It was tiresome but a welcome distraction to be asked for my help by my peers. I think it helped me as much as my group. It forced me to think about my own past in a different light. As I became better at helping them navigate their messes, I became better at helping myself through mine. I don't take credit for my friends healing processes; I was thankful to them for choosing me to help end their silent suffering. I was grateful that *they* helped *me*. At least the healing process had started. For them and for me.

Chapter 18

Epic Fail

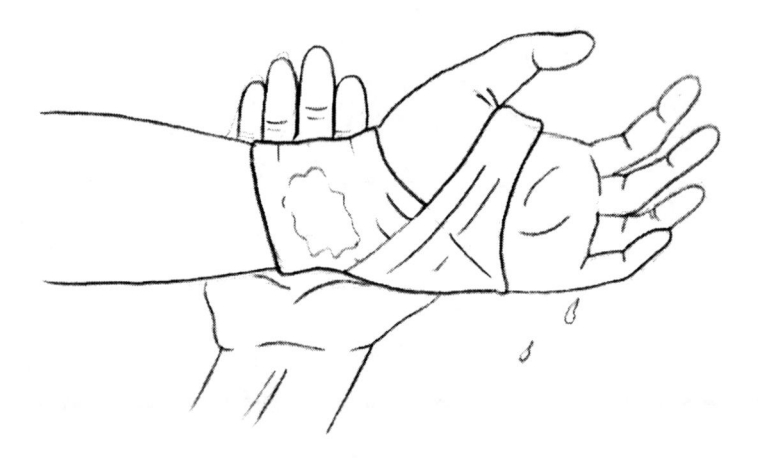

Since I wasn't in the psych facility for "drug abuse", I was able to go home for a few hours at a time. I made sure I brought at least a few joints, and pill-popping drugs to sneak back in with me; small stuff that was easily hidden, and generally safe for a small decent buzz. I hid them in various slits I made in my clothes so they would be undetected by the staff. As wrong as it sounds, the drugs were my "in" with some of the kids. If I shared a little treat here and there, the other kids trusted me even more. They didn't feel threatened by me like they did by the doctors and psych techs. We were equals. We were all screwed up. It also gave me a sense of power, and accomplishment to outsmart the staff. It never occurred to me that I became a drug dealer to unstable, and possibly over-medicated juveniles.

At outdoor recreational time, the male psych techs put the girls in a locked tennis court, and they would go play football with the guys. We never played tennis, we mostly just sat around, talked and smoked. We had a great time; just talking, and acting like teen age fools. I came to care deeply about my new friends. They were incredible and fascinating. I could never explain the feelings I held, watching them slowly heal, little by little. Most of the people I met in there changed drastically for the better. I decided I was almost glad Mom and Dad dropped me in there.

The football field was far enough away that they couldn't see what we were doing, but close enough that if we hollered, they could hear us. We would all light a cigarette at once, and sneak hits off a joint in between. It was crazy, because other than the night of being admitted, I was never screened for drugs again.

After I was there for about five weeks I received a weekend release to go home with an ankle monitor. I was so excited. I could sleep in my own bed, and Mom took a whole weekend off work so we could spend time together. Dad's insurance only covered a six week stay, and it was up in a week. So the docs thought it was time for me to get used to a little bit of a routine at home.

Mom picked me up as planned, and on the ride home we talked about what we would do over the weekend. We were both giddy with excitement, and incredibly happy to have this time together. I was only allowed to go so far from the house, so games, cards, and visitors was our plan. Gage was over for the weekend, I was overwhelmed with gratitude to be able to visit with him as well. It was like a breath of fresh air.

We pulled into the driveway, and Gage came out to meet us. I started to get out of the car, but stopped when I saw the expression on his face. He charged at us savagely, hollering loud enough for the whole block to hear. I couldn't understand what he was saying because he was talking so fast, but the angry look on his face told me he was enraged. It was clear from his purposeful stride toward me and upraised fist, that I was the target of his outburst. He was headed straight for me. I slammed the door, shut the window, and locked the door just as he reached my side of the car. He screamed at me through the window, and pounded on it with his fists.

I had no problem understanding what he was saying anymore. Sprays of spit sprayed across the glass, two inches from my face as he screamed obscenities at me. He didn't want me there. My brother did not want me to come back home…ever!

He spewed hateful, bitter insults at me. He let me know that everything that ever wrong in our lives was my fault. He hated me, and never wanted anything to do with me again. Mom was trying desperately to calm him down--to get him to listen to reason. He kept yelling, and wouldn't stop. I burst into hot, humiliated tears, and I begged my mom to take me back. Our weekend was shattered.

I felt the gut wrenching pain as his words became a sledge hammer, thrown through my window, feeling it shatter as slithers of glass flew everywhere. My window pane was no longer intact; it was shattered beyond repair, leaving nothing to protect me from the outside world. Mom and I drove back to the psych unit, crying, unable to say a word. My wonderful weekend home was over, and I never even left the car.

I pounded on the buzzer to alert the guard nurse that I was at the door. Pounding hard, as I sobbed uncontrollably. She let me back in, and I made a beeline straight to my room without stopping. I didn't acknowledge anyone's questioning looks or shouts of, "What's wrong?" I was hurt, and madder than I had ever been in my life.

Accusations ran through my mind faster than lightening. Each one came with a stab to my heart, blurred in my race for safety. *Gage told Mom about Grandpa*, he didn't doubt me then. Now he actually believed I enjoyed it. In my daze, and disappointment, it took me a few minutes to register the true source of Gage's contempt of me. It hit me like a bolt of lightning...Joey and Alfred - the grand premiere showing of my acting debut. Gage hated me because he saw me smiling while have sex with Joey and Alfred. Gage believed my act, and honestly thought I was a slut. I had hoped Gage saw through my clumsy acting, and somehow knew that I was not a willing participant in that threesome. My own brother thought I was enjoying it. My brother! I realize that I should hate *him* for not knowing me better... for not believing in me despite the twisted evidence against me. He never questioned me about any of it. I assumed he knew the truth. We always a close relationship growing up, right up until he saw me sprawled under my rapists, doing what I was forced to do to survive. He was supposed to protect me, not accuse me.

The sand storm of thoughts rushed in waves through my mind. I was a fucking baby who was brutally raped, tortured, and scarred for years by four...FOUR disgusting pigs! What did I ever do to deserve any of this shit? At that moment, I hated my brother. I hated my father, my grandfather, and that son of a bitch Alfred. I even hated Joey. I hated them all...but most of all I hated myself. I was not strong enough, smart enough, and too stupid for not saying no loud enough. I was the reason everyone was torn to pieces, and it was my fault my mom was so hurt. I was the one who couldn't stop the monsters from ripping my body apart. It was me, and me alone who destroyed everyone. The weight was too heavy to carry. I could not bear the burden any longer, I refused to stick around, and feel the torturous rage within me.

I charged to my room, and barricaded the door with a chair. Eve was out on the floor, so I was alone, with the exception of the techs yelling at my door. I quickly pulled the wire from my therapy notebook, and started carving at my wrist, from the inside down. I would rip myself to shreds on my own, and I would do it right. I was ready, hungry to see my own blood for the last time. Wanting my death more than I ever wanted anything before.

I didn't get deep enough before the psych techs broke down the door. I gouged as hard as I could at my wrist, but one would not be enough. I started to throw things at them while my wrist was bleeding. I fought hard, kicking, and screaming the entire time. Anything and everything to keep them from stopping me. I shattered the chair on the window, forgetting it was bullet proof. I fought. I fought for all the battles I ever faced and lost, against all of the incest, rapes, and beatings. I battled against all the bullies who never got what was coming to them. I screamed against my own self-loathing. It felt good to make contact with anything – the bed, the window, or the wall. It felt good to hurt someone else, and even better to hurt myself. I battled as though my very sanity depended on it.

It took three guys to take me down; this included both Mark and Brad. Tears stung at my face as I felt myself hit the ground. Sobbing and begging to finish what I started. One tech got me down on the floor, Brad and Mark grabbed my shoulders as they all hauled me to another room. Mark was whispering in my ear to calm down, to breathe, making the motions with me as they dressed the wound on my wrist. He tried desperately to talk me off the slippery edge I walked. I fought and sobbed against it until they had a firm grip on my hand. I was a far cry from done. I raged at them to let me go, as they attempted to bandage me up. Squirming and fighting every step of the way. I had a lot more cold-blood surging through my veins.

They put me in a room with a large punching bag, and

glove's. It was padded all the way around. I didn't bother with the gloves. I needed to feel my bare skin making contact with something hard, and unyielding. I needed to feel as though I was really punishing it. Every time I threw a punch or a kick, there was the face of one of my abusers on the receiving end. I punched, and kicked the bag until my knuckles bled freely. I was exhausted. I sat down, and sobbed uncontrollably, bleeding from my wrist once again. I kept trying to force more blood out, as much as possible. I bore my nails into the wound in order to finish what I started. Blood started to flow freely from my injured wrist, but it wasn't deep enough. I didn't feel the physical pain--just an empty, used up bitterness in the pit of my stomach.

    The psych techs were perched by the door ready to dart in if I hurt myself too badly, but they knew I needed to do battle with my demons. When they knew I was spent, my friend and psych tech, Brad came in the door. He quietly coaxed me to say a word or two. Desperately trying to start my healing process once again.

    Slowly, one painful word after another, I told him what happened, and he said he understood why I broke down. We talked until I couldn't cry anymore. He was a great counselor. He even got a little smile out of me. We walked down to the gym, we shot basketball hoops, and played "HORSE" a couple of times. We talked; he wanted to know more, but I wanted peace. Brad reminded me of the horrible things that happened to me. The broken trusts, violent intrusions, and my guilt for things that were out of my control. He kept reminding me that they didn't define me. They made me stronger, wiser, and brave. It would drive me to be the person I want to be, if I learned to control it, and understand it.

SHATTERED PANE

After that, I was put on suicide watch for a few days. The couch became my bed, and a nurse watched over me at night. My psychiatrist recommended that I not be released at that point. I was too vulnerable, and was at a high risk of attempting to take my life again. The insurance wouldn't cover anything past six weeks, and my parents fought. Dad thought I should be fixed after six whole weeks of therapy. He was part of the reason I was there, but was blind to that fact. Mom didn't have the money, but she did more for me than he ever could have imagined, she was actually my drive to succeed.

Mom knew better. She refused to even entertain the idea of my getting out. Since the insurance was in Dad's name, and he signed me in, he was held accountable for all payments. Not only was he financially responsible for the payments for my mental healthcare…he was a key player in the need for it.

After a few days, I regained some of my wit. I started to get my determination back, and fell back into my routine on the floor. My friends were there for me, never judging, and never denying the truth. I was doing well, and functioning properly. I knew I had to go home at some point, but I didn't want to. I was safe from harassment there, no one blamed me or tried to hurt me. I was safe, and I liked it. It's amazing how a psychiatric ward could make you comfortable, and secure when your own family scares you the most.

For the next two weeks I spent many hours in counseling sessions processing the rage, and hatred that exploded out of me. I held it for years. That's when I started to change. The empowerment I discovered made a huge impact on my life. I learned firsthand that the bottled up guilt, and shame that ran through my veins had been ruining me from the inside out for a long time. It festered and grew until it could not be contained by the delicate membranes, and scars that covered it. The fear and anger had to be bled out. Letting go of it allowed me to begin to truly heal…at least enough to survive myself. I decided I would no longer let guilt or shame overrule my mind or heart. I was the one betrayed by the people I loved, and trusted the most. By the ones who were supposed to love, and protect me. I was the one who was taken advantage of, tricked into doing things little girls shouldn't do. I was not a whore; it was not my fault. I reminded myself of that often, constantly repeating it in my mind until I could feel my confidence return.

 I did return home after eight weeks. It was a hard adjustment. Gage lived with my dad, so unless he decided to visit, which wasn't often, I felt safe. I didn't think he would hurt me, but given my history with men, I thought it'd be wise to take the "better safe than sorry" approach. If he did come, I made sure to lock myself in my room or go walk the subdivision so he wouldn't have to see me.

Chapter 19

Busted

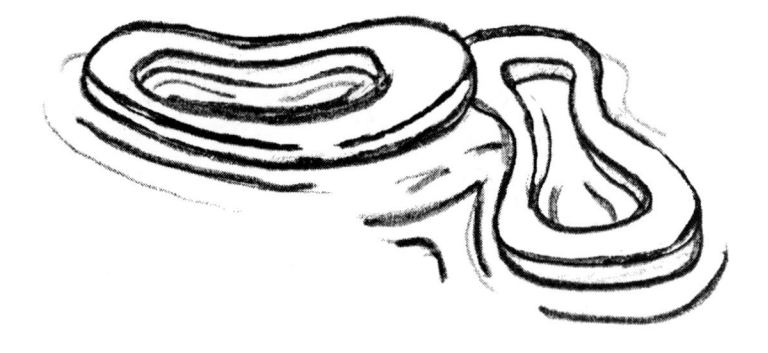

Eventually, Gage and I got used to seeing each other. We were close enough in age that we had a lot of mutual friends. I hung out at the same party spot he did when he was home. Mom was working a lot, so sneaking out wasn't difficult. I went out the side door, and she never knew. I knew it was selfish of me. I took advantage of Mom's long work hours, and I did feel guilty sometimes, but not enough to skip a party. After a while things calmed down between Gage and I. He didn't scowl when he saw me, and I didn't feel the need to disappear when he was around. We co-existed on the weekends he was home, and I partied with, and without him. Things went along fine until Mom discovered my habits of drinking all night, and she told Gage to nail my window closed. It slowed me down, but not for long. She forgot to nail the side door shut.

She was incredibly angry one night when I came home drunk. She waited up for me when she realized I wasn't in my bed. She'd had enough. Gage was home that weekend and stood up for me in his own way. I was drunk and high, so I sat on the bed awaiting my punishment while Mom and Gage had a screaming match. Then Mom marched in my room, and began to pack my bags to go to Dad's. Gage said I wasn't going. She pulled something out of my dresser to put in my suitcase, and Gage pulled the clothes from my suitcase, and put them back. It was quite amusing, and I had to work hard to stifle my drunken laughter. Eventually, they both gave up, and we all went to bed. After I sobered up, I realized I pushed my mother to her limit, and I decided I better lay off the partying for a while and be a good girl. In my heart of hearts, I knew she would never send me to live with my dad. A person could only handle so much. I never knew if the reason Gage was so adamant about my staying with Mom was because he was concerned for my safety, or for his privacy. After all, he lived at Dad's the majority of the time. It didn't matter to me. All that mattered is that I had a reprieve.

I finally turned sixteen and got my driver's license as soon as I could. Dad helped a bit towards a down payment on a used black Subaru. The rest I borrowed from my Uncle Garrett and Aunt Paige. We worked out an agreement with payments at $100 a month until it was paid off.

I already had a job as a waitress. It became easier after I had my own car. I enjoyed the work; liked talking to the customers, and felt a sense of satisfaction from helping Mom out with the bills. It felt good to able to help her for once.

I was sixteen when my little brother Braden was born. Just like with Angel, Dad decided to pull me out of school to take me to see him. The difference was that I wasn't there that day. I skipped school to go tubing at Culver Rider Park. There was a bridge there. We dropped huge tubes in the water, jumped the one story length, and landed in the tubes. The thrill of the drop was exhilarating. My adrenaline was pumped.

When I arrived home later that day, I was in trouble. I was also told this little miracle was born. I was allowed to go visit, but had to come straight back home. I was off work that day from my waitressing job. My mom was disappointed that I skipped school once again. She understood the sadness I was going through, so she let this one slide. I still managed straight A's, but was set back on my GPA due to low grades from the psych unit.

I went up to the hospital and saw this brand new precious little life. There is something about the soft sweetness of a new-born baby that always put a smile on my face. Braden seemed so tiny with a head full of dark brown, wild hair. It stood up everywhere. He had the newborn squinty eyes along with soft chubby cheeks. He smelled of the innocence all babies have--the smell that would bring a smile to anyone's stone cold smirk. I guess it didn't help that I was biase; this was my sweet little brother. Swaddled tight in a thin baby blanket. He was soft and sleeping as innocent babies should; I was in awe of him.

I had been depressed due to female issues. I was recently told I had severe Endometriosis and ovulating cysts on my ovaries. It was likely that I would never conceive a child. Braden's sweet tiny face, brought all that forward. I would never be able to look down, and gush with pride for my own child, for it wasn't meant to be.

Chapter 20

Blind Love

I met Ray at the age of sixteen; he was twenty-six. He was one of my first boyfriends, and I thought he walked on water. We met through Mia, my brother's girlfriend. We had an instant connection, or at least I did. He was gorgeous at six foot tall, fit, tanned with dirty blond hair and blue eyes. He was big, and burly with arms as thick as tree trunks. He oozed quiet confidence, but that was the only quiet thing about him. His voice was gruff, his laughter boomed, but his words were always sweet to me. When he spoke I hung on his every word. He mesmerized, and fascinated me. He swept me off my feet.

He was considerate and caring. It didn't take long before I had fallen head over heels in love with him. He was mysterious, and complicated, had a passion for music, and a soft side he reserved just for me. We sat for hours as he played the guitar and sang to me, both of us getting high on the sweet melodies that drifted through his fingers.

We both enjoyed a common enemy. We both abused drugs. It didn't seem wrong when we did it together. I trusted his judgment as to what and how much to use. He was much more experienced at things than I was.

We kept our smoky haze pretty well hidden from Mom, and she liked Ray too. She thought he was a bit too old for me, but she sensed a protective nature about him, and felt I would be safe with him. Possibly just a passing phase, a teenage crush.

Mom, Ray, and I were on our way home from dinner as a horrible news report came on the radio. A tornado hit the town we lived in, right in Aunt Sara's condominium complex, as well as the apartment buildings where Gage and Mia recently moved.

We raced there and reached Aunt Sara's complex first. We arrived before the first responders. The condos were a disaster. Almost all the roofs were off; some were torn in half, and some leveled. As I looked to my right, one home caught my eye. The upper level was gone, and all that stood was a lonely empty crib. I scanned quickly for a baby, and saw what I assumed was the crib's occupant with his family sitting on the stoop next door. They were tightly clutching their infant and staring blankly at the half of the condo that remained.

We found Sara and the girls on their porch. The two women hugged tightly, Mom checking over her sister and nieces making sure they weren't hurt. Once Mom was convinced they were fine, she left me with them to help and headed down the road to check on my brother. Ray went with her. I helped clear the rubble as much as I could, but there was so much debris and pieces of peoples' lives scattered everywhere it didn't seem to make much of a difference. We all worked together, moving rubble to free occupants from their homes.

The road was blocked so Mom parked her car on the side of the street. She and Ray headed, on foot, through the field that led to the complex. They found them quickly, and determined that they were ok. The apartment buildings hadn't sustained nearly as much damage as the condos. Aunt Sara, the girls, and I were ushered onto a bus. They were taking the victims to safe shelters. As we drove away, I surveyed the complex; I thought it was a miracle that no one was killed.

Ray and Mom found us at one of the shelters. I tucked myself into Ray's arms and shivered at the thought of what could have happened. He held me tight and softly kissed my

SHATTERED PANE

forehead. I relaxed, and rested my head on his broad shoulders. It felt good. I was positive he could, and would, fight off a tornado to protect me.

Ray and I connected emotionally, physically, and soulfully in a way that sent my senses spinning. I never experienced any hint of sexual desire towards anyone before; the heat I felt when he touched me was new and exhilarating. His caresses were a welcome delight to my body. I was skilled in the art of escaping the world during sex, but naïve at being fully present in the moment; to the pleasures it evoked. It was a completely new experience to look into my lover's eyes, and want more--need more. He awakened a fire in me that I never dreamed existed.

Ray taught me that sex should never be painful or forced. Despite knowing that in my logical mind, I could never believe it, not in my heart of hearts. Therapy couldn't erase my experiences or my hatred of sex. Even after years of therapy, I still believed part of being a girl meant I would be on the receiving end of whatever sexual hell a man wanted to put me through. Ray changed that. His strokes were gentle, his tongue soft, and his caresses held nothing but warmth and love. He was careful, taking extra measures to make sure I was not hurt mentally or physically. He knew I was afraid of the dark, so he made sure there was always a soft glow of light. When I opened my eyes, I saw his face. He scoured mine for any sign of anything less than pleasure. We shared an intimacy and bond I had never known. It became my reality, and I found a life I never knew existed.

Ray and I dated for two years, I was completely head over heels in love with him. He could do no wrong in my eyes. It was blind love; no matter what his faults were, I could easily excuse them away in my mind. A day didn't go by that he didn't have a sweet compliment for me. He'd tell me I was the most beautiful when I first woke up in the morning, hair disheveled, without a smidge of make-up. He always told me I was the smartest person he knew. He said all the things a woman in love wanted to hear, and he meant every word of it; things I'd never heard from any man in my life. It was overwhelmingly perfect.

I asked for a camera for Christmas, and begged for him to let me open it early so I could use it to take family pictures on Christmas day. He relented, but when I opened the box it wasn't a camera, it was an engagement ring, placed in a camera box. Right then and there he asked me to marry him. Without a doubt in my mind, I said yes. Then he gave me my camera so I could use it for Christmas. I was giddy with delight, nothing could bust my bubble.

I graduated high school on Friday, June 1, and was married on Sunday June 3, 1990. We held an outdoor wedding and the weather couldn't have been more perfect. Both my parents walked me down the aisle and both told me we could turn around and have the party without the wedding. I knew they didn't want me marrying him, but I had never been so sure about anything in my entire life. Besides, Dad didn't get to have a say in my life, and I didn't believe my mom had ever known a love this deep.

Our marriage started off well. We got along great; he was my best friend, the person I told everything to, and looked to for support and comfort. He was my rock. My new foundation for all my hopes, and dreams to come true.

SHATTERED PANE

One of his favorite things to do was to take me hunting, dressing me up in camouflage clothes. I loved watching his giggle turn into a roaring belly laugh while he painted my face. He kissed and hugged me constantly, never dropping my hand when we were together. He was proud of me, and always made sure everyone knew I was his. I never felt a sense of pride from any man in my life, and I loved it.

Instead of taking a honeymoon, we used the $4000.00 we received as wedding gifts to buy a used rundown trailer. Ray was a carpenter by trade, and planned to fix it up so we could call it a home. My dad stopped by to take a look at it, and give us his advice on what we needed to do to fix it up. He pointed out that the carpet was infested with fleas. A major issue we had overlooked. We weren't sure what to do, all our money had gone to purchasing the trailer. Dad said if we ripped the carpet out he would pay for the new carpet as part of our wedding gift. So we fumigated, tore all the carpet out, and fumigated it again.

I called my dad when the carpet was out, cleaned up, and the trailer was moved to our lot. I believe I shocked him; he explained that there was not enough money in his budget for carpet for our trailer. No apology, no regret…nothing. He was lying, and I knew it. He probably bought one of his other kids a fancy present with the money he was supposed to give to me. Ray witnessed the arrangements, so I knew I couldn't be called a liar.

My Uncle Garrett and Aunt Paige just had their floors redone and offered us the old carpet. It came from three different rooms and was three different colors. Burgundy, light blue, and green. Not having a better idea, we thanked them graciously, and tried to make it work the best we could. None of the pieces were big enough to cover the living room floor so we patched the two biggest pieces together, and did the best with what we had. There was enough of the green carpet to *almost* fit the bedroom. It was a sight to see. It was not the nice caramel cream carpet we picked out in the carpet store, but at least it didn't have bugs.

The walls were covered with dark paneling that made the room seem sad and gloomy. Ray came home from a job site one day with a truck load of drywall. He hung and taped it in the living room. Little by little we renovated what we could as we got a little money. Progress was slow, and it wasn't a head turner, but it was a home, nonetheless. Ray continued to work construction as I ran my tail off waiting tables, going to college, and working a full time job as an editor. I made good tips, but I worked hard for them, bending over backwards to please my customers, and smiling until my face hurt.

Ray's brother, Andrew, decided to make the move from New York, and Ray graciously offered our spare bedroom. He had no job, but he was family now, so I felt compelled to welcome him into our home. He arrived driving an old jeep, stuffed with everything he owned in the world. It wasn't much. Ray got him hired on with the man he worked for, but I learned quickly that Andrew wasn't the working type. In fact, I began to discover that Ray wasn't as hard working as I thought either. They gradually began spending more time at home playing with their bows and arrows than going to work.

Andrew was definitely not a good influence on my husband, and I resented him for it. They were both lazy, and

SHATTERED PANE

never cleaned up their mess. I never noticed how much of a slob Ray was before then, but I definitely noticed it after busting my ass working a double shift to pay the electric bill. My home was filled with dirty dishes everywhere, food bowls used as ashtrays, sour milk on the counter, and so much trash on the floor you couldn't walk to the hall or the bedroom. They were both always laid off or not working due to the weather, or whatever excuse was plausible.

One day when they were at home, and had nothing better to do, they rigged up a target at the end of the hall by the bedrooms. They stood in the kitchen, shot arrows the length of our home, through the open decorative window to the living room, and into the target. I walked in as an arrow whizzed by me, landing directly in the bull's eye of the target. The boys yelled, "Watch out!" high-fived each other, and reloaded. Simple and innocent as if every person they ever knew had already done it. I couldn't believe my eyes, but I was too tired to argue. I waited until the coast was clear and went straight to bed. I was still in college thanks to a few grants.

I waitressed on the weekends to make up for the money we owed for bills. I no longer kept my nicotine and pot only rule. I used speed or crystal to keep me going through the day and dope or downers to sleep during the nights. I still had nightmares at night, but Ray was always there to comfort me. He held me until they passed.

I no longer held onto the grand illusion of a perfect marriage, but I still loved Ray whole-heartedly. Nobody is perfect. I forgave him for all his laziness and disgusting habits routinely. He might not have given me what I hoped for, but he gave me what I needed most…his love; and I loved him back without reservation. Our marriage was only surviving on the love we had for each other.

However, love doesn't pay the bills, and we were flat broke. At one point in college, I was short $80 on books. I worked, paid the rent, paid for my car, and paid the remainder on my classes. Yet, I could not come up with that last $80. I knew Mom didn't have it; Grandma Eden had no money; but I asked them nonetheless. Even between the three of us, we could not pull the money together in time.

I just needed a loan for two weeks, until Ray's check came in. He was working a little at that time. I went against my gut and called Dad. I barely had time to explain the situation before he turned me down. He said that I was the one who decided to get married; it was time I gave up my dream of graduating, and should go to work like a normal adult. I was hurt, but not surprised. I should have known better.

I was frustrated by my lack of funds for books. I was a damn hard worker, holding down two jobs, and going to school too! It was harder than I ever imagined; I hoped my dad might just be proud of me and help me out a little. I was disappointed he refused to part with $80. That was play money to him, but it was a life raft to me…and he knew it. I knew from that point on I would never, ever ask my father for anything again, even if it meant I starved to death.

Digging hard and deep, Grandma, Mom and I, scraped the money together, using change and a check that we knew would bounce. We'd pay the bounced check fees with Ray's check. We had always robbed Peter to pay Paul, and I learned a few tricks to survive.

SHATTERED PANE

Ray went to school for over the road truck driving, and in between semesters, I took off work and went with him. His brother went to live with his parents about two hours away. I guess he needed somebody else to mooch off. We were gone six weeks at a time, and home for a week, then we would do it again. We trucked all over the United States. Those were some of the fondest memories I have of our time together. We were the kind of couple who thrived on being with each other 24/7. There was never a shortage of conversation, and the cab of his truck was roomy enough for some pretty steamy lovemaking. Somewhere between California and Oklahoma we fell even more in love. We bonded and became so close, I felt as though our hearts were meshed together. He knew everything about me, except for some of the more horrific details, and still chose to love me anyway.

We took time out in different states, sightseeing as much as possible. I loved learning the details about all the places we went. I was thrilled, and amazed to discover the beauty of the flatlands, the mountains, and the dessert. It was an incredible adventure.

One of my favorite stops was the Grand Canyon Little River Gorge. We inched our way up the winding roads, many of them being a hair shy of being too thin for our big rig. We stopped at a safe pathway and parked the truck. We ran to the guard rail, leaned over as far as safety would permit, and admired the view. It was breath taking, with the vast array of slopes, and an incredible depth in which only God could provide. It was the most beautiful natural landmark I had ever seen.

Since we were on the road so much, we decided to sell the trailer, and move in with Mom. The basement was already finished. It didn't make sense to keep the trailer, and we could use the money. Unfortunately, Ray's truck driving career lasted less than two years. After our journey across America, I guess he felt like there was nothing left to see. The job no longer held the thrill for him that it used to, and he became bored with it all. I didn't mind being back at home with Mom; I loved getting to spend time with her again.

Ray went back to construction, and I decided to continue my education. I thought it was a good idea to get a quick start on my career, and get a certificate from a Tech school. Once again, I worked and took college courses at the same time, but I got my certificate as a Certified Laboratory Technologist. I graduated with a 99.9%. I was named Valedictorian of my class.

I was prepared to go to work and was excited about my new career. I landed a great position a job working in the Microbiology Lab at St. Clair Hospital. I worked 40 hours a week so we would have health insurance. I continued my studies, too, carrying fifteen credit hours of college courses and held a part time waitressing job on my free nights and weekends. I begrudgingly took on the tiring role of primary breadwinner for our family again, as Ray fell back into bad habits.

It was easy to get back into drugs, and once again Ray was constantly unemployed. It was hard to make ends meet, even living in Mom's basement. He was a squanderer of money; he didn't have the understanding of being a good provider. We didn't see each other much during that time. When he had a job, he worked it. When he didn't, he hunted. He hunted *a lot* more than he worked.

Chapter 21

Gifts

We weren't home long before someone else needed our help. Someone we cared for was in trouble, so Mom opened her home once again. This time it was a close family friend, Sadie, and her two year old daughter, Alex, who was our Goddaughter. Sadie was in an abusive relationship and decided to leave her boyfriend. She was small and thin. Her light blue eyes were always bright, surrounded by a golden tan, and hair that looked sun-kissed which complemented her skin nicely.

I snuck her and her baby out of her trailer one night while her boyfriend was asleep. The door woke him up to find her gone. We hadn't made it out of eyesight when he came out of the door with a gun and started shooting. We bolted to the car, shielding the baby with our bodies, and sped away a split second ahead of one of his bullets.

We couldn't offer them much more than a safe place to sleep and food in their bellies, but they were comfortable. Sadie quickly made herself at home, so much so that she slept with my husband.

After five years of marriage, Ray had an affair with that skinny bitch in our bed! I was destroyed. With no warning or tell-tale signs of a marriage on the rocks, he popped up with the news that he was no longer in love with me. At 5' 4" and a 125 pounds, I was too fat for him; I wasn't desirable to him anymore. Oh, and he never wanted to have children; the children he knew I desperately longed to try for.

Before my head even stopped spinning, he left with her… and her child. They moved out quickly, loaded her car, and went back to New York. Their home-wrecking infatuation lasted a mere two weeks.

The first thing I did was to buy my mom and I new mattresses. I couldn't stand the thought of sleeping in a bed in which my husband had sex with another woman. Then, I became paralyzed. Seven years with him, and he threw it all away for what? A shallow, bony, husband-stealing whore who was good for fourteen days of hot sex.

My world collapsed around me. It was as if the tornado from years ago, ripped through town again, and ripped everything I loved away from me with it. I was devastated. My heart literally ached from his betrayal. I was incapable of even processing what happened. I replayed the whole seven years in my head over, and over again, trying to figure out what I had done wrong. When exactly did I get too fat for him? He spent years convincing me how beautiful I was, never noticing the small faded burn marks on my face. He kissed the scars of my battered body a thousand times, trying to erase the hurt and humiliation they brought me.

Over the years, and with help, I was able to bring some of my fragile shards of window glass back together. Slowly and painfully lining the edge of the pane together. The razor sharp pieces were like a puzzle, I searched for the outside pieces first and worked my way in. I had come so far with it, only to have him clear the edges again for a quick get-away.

Every lash, gash, and burn put together didn't come close the depth of the wounds inflicted on my heart, as Ray casually discarded me like a toy that he got tired of. I wracked my brain to make sense of what my world had become. I overcome so much indescribable pain that my monsters inflicted on me as a child, only to be shattered beyond repair by the one man who ever showed me love. We knew each other

SHATTERED PANE

inside and out; I thought I knew him, but maybe my need for love clouded my view so much I couldn't see the truth. Did he ever love me? I began to doubt the truth I knew about us. I trusted him. I gave him every part of me without reservation. I exposed everything good and bad of my fragile heart to him. Did he just feel sorry for me? Did he get his own sense of twisted pleasure from trying to "fix me"?

I felt as though I was drowning in a sea of heartbreak. My dad even tried to talk to me on several occasions. He reminded me that some things can catch you out of the blue, and that it was okay to feel hurt and angry. He also made sure I knew that I couldn't stay there long. At some point, I would have to pick myself up, and go on with my life.

Mom was ready to kill. She couldn't stand the sight or thought of him. Even his name brought out a rage in her in which she couldn't control. He wounded her baby incredibly. She did everything in her power to help me. She made me my favorite dinners, offered whatever advice she could come up with, but she was as bewildered as I was.

I started hanging out with my friends more, going out, and yes, still drinking and using drugs. I received plenty of offers for dates. In the beginning, I turned them all down. I didn't feel ready. I continued my position working in the Microbiology Lab, went to college in the evenings, and waitressed on the weekends. With a full schedule, it left me little time to grieve.

I was incredibly lucky to have my friends in my life. My mom, Amy, and I all sat down one night, and burned pictures of him. It was liberating. My friends always had my back. Brittney, Amy, Rob, Jerry, Bryan, and Jared were my biggest support during that time. I know it was hard on them; he was their friend also.

A good friend, Lonny, asked me out. I'd known him for a long time. I accepted. I didn't want to give him a bad impression, so I tried to note that it was as friends only. I wasn't ready for anything more. It was an incredible evening. We went to dinner and to the movies. He was sweet, and caring. We talked a lot, and ended the night on good terms.

Soon after, I received several date requests. I started saying yes. I was exposed to new restaurants, personalities, and places. I started enjoying it. Although it was nice to be wined and dined, none of them made my heart flutter, so the dates always ended easily.

I was trying desperately to file for divorce. A simple uncontested divorce. I decided to do it myself; money was tight, and I had no way of paying a lawyer. Most of the paperwork was done, but Ray would not sign. He was out of state, and I learned I could place ads in the paper. If they were unanswered after a specified time period, I was free to move forward on my own with the divorce.

Christmas was coming up, and I had all my presents bought. I found the perfect gift for Dad and Diana and was excited to give it to them. At that point, Angel and Braden were easy to please with the latest and greatest toy on the market.

Soon after, dad called. He tried to explain that Christmas was about the children, and he thought this Christmas he would do things differently. We would spend time as a family, but gifts would only be bought for the kids; Angel and Braden. He claimed money was tight, and they didn't have enough to go around. I hesitantly agreed.

After much thought, I realized that every gift he ever given us was a $25 check or a couple of socks or shirts. Gage and I were still his children too. So I called him back, told him I already gotten their gift, and it could not be returned. I let him know how I felt, that although we were not kids, we were still his kids. So he agreed to the gift exchange. Christmas came, and we shared it at their house.

It didn't take long to realize why they were short on money. Angel was head over heels about the new computer, and all the stuff that went with it that she received for Christmas. Braden was all for showing off all of his brand new Hockey equipment including new skates, pads, helmet, and large duffle bag to carry it all in. Gage and I got the same check as always. After all, that was all they could afford with the new house. If he thought my mom's gifts equaled Angel and Braden's, then I would think their gifts should equal $100. Not $500.

Dad used this logic of his pitiful gifts; we also had a mother whom was buying us gifts as well. Gage and I had two parents as well as Angel and Braden. My mom tried desperately to put us first and foremost. She gave us her time, love, and patience. I never complained over anything she offered. Money was tight, barely enough to feed and clothe us, much less buy gifts. She succeeded every year without fail. Gifts were bought and wrapped, dinners were made, and we spent our time together. My mother's strength never faltered in front of me. She's the most amazing person I have ever known.

I was incredibly happy that Angel and Braden were being raised the way they were meant to be. That is what our agreement was all about. It wasn't about the money or gifts. All I ever wanted was to feel as though he cared, that I was equal to his other children, and that he still loved me. I never got any of that. I will never forget Angel's little smile, bright innocent eyes, and her bouncy curls when she ran to greet me at the door every time.

Braden, with his deep dark brown eyes, and his straight brown hair. Ran around with so much energy and thrill, that he could never concentrate on one thing at a time. His spirit was boundless as he tried to master whatever he set out to do.

I truly believe my sister and brother were in the perfect family. Being raised as normal kids are, given the love, and attention they deserved. Angel loved school, and always talked about the normal girlfriend/boyfriend drama that was going on in her life. It was refreshing to hear. I could see the excitement in her eyes, and hear the frustration in her voice. I never had to wonder what she was thinking; her face mirrored whatever emotion she felt. It was beyond her control, and incredibly entertaining to watch.

Braden was an incredibly reckless young boy. He never took the time to think things through, to weigh the risks involved with the adventures he tried. Consequences never crossed his mind. He was a true boy, was my opinion. I could see his mind spin as he conjured up his next quest, his brain struggled with how to make it work in the most thrilling way possible. Although my family may think I have petty problems with Dad, I would rather them think it was my problem, than his. Angel truly is, and always has been "Daddy's little girl". That was my ultimate goal.

Chapter 22

That Goose

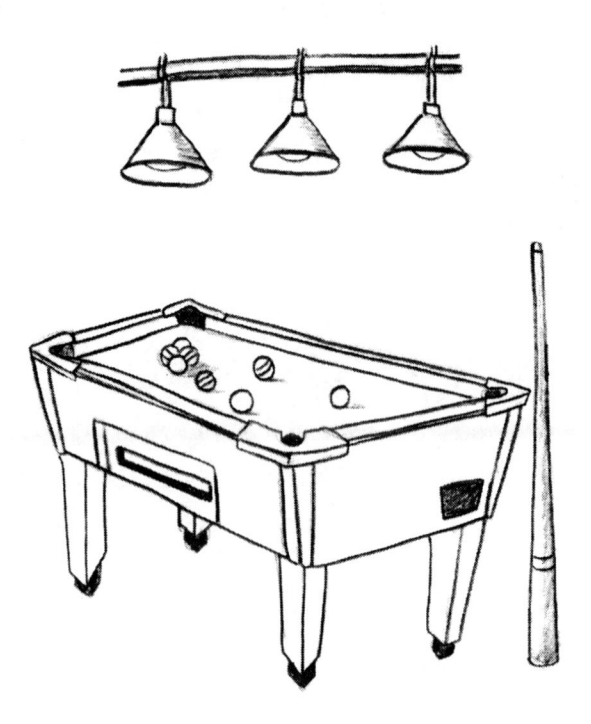

The doctor's discovered that my grandmother's cancer returned and had metastasized throughout several vital organs. They only gave her three months to live. She made her decision then and there. She was tired of fighting and constantly being ill. Cancer had invaded her body six times before. With each one, she battled it like a champ. This time, she chose not to start therapy and was simply thankful for the life she lived.

We were all continuously at her house helping her with her daily needs, and cooking for Grandpa. A hospital bed took the place of the couch in their living room. She amazingly kept her humor intact, battling the depression it brought on. The family would sit around and visit. Grandma was comical, high on various pain meds as we laughed throughout the days.

We watched as she slowly deteriorated before our eyes. It wasn't long before she was bedridden and placed on hospice to manage her pain. Morphine was a constant in her life. She could lay pain free in her bed and visit with family. She was wasting away quickly, her head was bald, and the life left her eyes.

Even in this state of mind she was loving, and amusing. She loved foot rubs and her family. She was never alone. Anyone who knew her, loved her deeply. People came from far and wide to say their goodbyes in person.

My beloved Grandmother died on March 12, 1995; three months and two days after her diagnosis. Her funeral was packed with people who loved her forever, and those she just met. She left a legacy in our lives. The procession of cars going to the cemetery was over a mile long. I had never seen so many cars behind, as we were first in line. I could not see the end.

I loved her as much as I did my own mother. She was my world, even though she stayed with my Grandfather. She was the most amazing person I had ever known. We were incredibly bonded by both hardship, and love. I always felt that I deserved a slow painful death. I felt as though it would make up for all the damage I had done to my loved ones. Somehow, I felt as though it was a cleansing, a preparation for whatever was to come next. Grandma had unbelievable faith; she prayed constantly and was completely committed to her religion. I felt in my heart that wherever she was going, she would never feel pain again. She is my guardian angel now, and forever. Things go wrong constantly, but she always makes sure we are safe in the end.

The following Friday, I was going to go home and take a shower. I had gotten off work and didn't have any classes that night. So, I thought I would relax and get some sleep. At this point, I was working 40 hours a week, taking college courses, and working part time waitressing at a bar. Sleep sounded pretty good. I wanted to stop by my mom's work and say hi first.

When I arrived, Mom told me that she and her friends were going for a few drinks at a bar called "That Goose". I quickly turned them down. However, Jane, the owner of the shop in which my mom worked, kept asking me to change my mind, so I relented and went. She wanted me to ride with her, so my mom drove my car. The whole drive over, she did nothing but talk about the two different dates she had that night. One at the bar, and one after the bar. All I had gotten were their names as I stared out the window in silence.

When we got there, we went in; it was incredibly packed

and extremely loud. All of the city water employees were there, and they were all men. The last thing I needed in my life was a man's attention. I was tired; Mom and her friends found a large table to sit at, they would most likely be there for the night.

Jane introduced me to a few of the guys, and I knew one of them was the one she was meeting there. I saw who he was, and she was right, he was incredibly handsome. I could see why she was excited. We all hung out for a while, until it was time for Jane to leave and meet the other guy. The only thing I knew for sure was that one was Bryan, and the other Kaden. With the bar being so loud, I couldn't hear the names of the people she introduced me to.

She left, and I went to join my mom and her friends. I was sitting there extremely tired, when I noticed the extremely handsome man she introduced me to. He was walking my way with my purse in his hand. I left it at the table when I moved. He asked if it was mine; I felt incredibly embarrassed, turning red as I retrieved it from his hand. I asked if he was busy, and if not, would he like to play a game of pool. He said yes, and that is what we did all night; drank beer, played pool, and talked. It was surprisingly fun; I enjoyed it. The beer started to kick in; I started to relax and enjoy his company. He caught my name, but at this point, I had yet to get his. I was curious, but felt it was extremely rude to ask.

He had an innocent sparkle in his beautiful hazel eyes. When the light hit them just right, hints of green jumped out. He had full, rich brown hair that looked as though it would be extremely soft and smooth to the touch. His smile set his whole face aglow. He was tall with wide, fit shoulders, a lean waist, and thighs. I was lost at the sight of him. He was a handsome man--the only man that held my attention in a long time.

We talked; he told me about his life, how he just graduated college, and was looking for a position in his field. Here was a college graduate, who actually had his life together. I had never met a man who had the manners, the degree, smart, funny, and cute, all in one package. He was completely down to earth. He intrigued me.

I never thought anyone of his caliber would be interested in me. I always attracted the bad boys, and paid for it later. I was comfortable in his presence, and didn't hesitate in sharing the drama I had been through in the past few years, including the fact that I was still doing crystal meth, and other drugs on occasion. Nor did I leave out the fact my ex was avoiding the divorce paperwork, and we had been separated a year and a half at that point. I didn't want to lead him astray, so honesty became my best policy. I wanted to leave him room for a swift easy get-away from this mad woman he just met. It was the first time in a long time I felt the tiniest shred of interest in a man, and it frightened me a little.

That is what I get for thinking. He actually asked me to meet him at another bar afterwards. I took a risk, accepted his phone number, and gave him mine in return. I asked if it was okay if I took a quick shower before meeting him again. He agreed, and we went our separate ways. I needed some time to clear my head. I had already drank more than my tolerance, so Mom drove home. As I hopped in the shower, she made me coffee so I could sober up before I met him again.

We waited for his call, and the phone rang, at the exact

time we agreed on. I had Mom answer the phone to try and get his name. We met up at a corner bar that was open for another hour and talked. It didn't feel right to stop where we left off, as the bar closed for the night. So since a breakfast restaurant was the only place open, that is where we went. He drove and was one of the sweetest men I ever met. He opened and closed my car door, held the door open for me, and never made an inappropriate comment. He drove, and I caught a glimpse of what a true gentleman was like. I was not used to this, but quickly decided I enjoyed.

It was like a whirlwind romance. We went out every night that week, and yes, I finally got his name. It was Kaden, and he was five days older than me. It didn't take long before I was introduced to his parents, George and Mary Livingston on March 31 at his dad's birthday party. It went well, but we hadn't mentioned my divorce held some issues, and was not yet finalized. I liked them a lot, and I felt as though they liked me as well.

It was time for Kaden to meet some of my family. I took him to meet my brother Gage, sister-in-law Mia, and my special niece Alana. Pronouncing my name was hard for her, I quickly became "Yaha" in her tiny little voice. She was three years old and hated men. She was the most precious little person in my life, and I was determined for her to like Kaden.

Kaden wanted to please her and be prepared. So we went to the store and loaded a basket filled with trinkets just for her. We left with flowers, balloons, candy, and trinkets I knew she would love.

When we walked into the living room, everyone was quickly introduced. Alana was hiding behind her Mom's legs, wondering who this man was I brought in her house. I coaxed her out a little at a time, and introduced her to Kaden. A small little scowl was on her face as she looked him up and down. Slowly, one by one he handed her the gifts. With each gift given, another step closer was taken. The vast array of balloons sealed the deal. Kaden was a hit.

He became her "Heaven", not mine. I took it as a good sign that Alana developed an immediate affinity for him. She wanted him all for herself. We were met with fierce eyes and a sharp tongue each time we got close or kissed. When we were apart, she quickly climbed on his lap, and told him about her day in her three year old sort of way. If I was over without Kaden, she was overjoyed that I was there. Kaden and I quickly came to the conclusion that since my Grandma Eden entered heaven a few days before we met, that our meeting was no coincidence. My grandmother and his grandmother had met quickly in the afterlife, and knew we both deserved a chance. With things stacked against us that evening, we still managed to meet and enjoyed each other's company immensely.

I knew in my head that I was not mentally ready for a relationship, yet there we were, a couple. I was not looking for a relationship, actually; it was something I was trying to avoid. I tried to push him away on several occasions. Even acting like a complete bitch didn't work.

I enjoyed our time together, but we were so different from each other. His heart was so pure, and innocent to the pains of the world. Mine had already been turned to stone. I didn't want to be the person to shatter his optimistic view of the world. I didn't even feel worthy of his attention to be honest, and I believed he would run anyway as soon as he discovered the person inside of me. I didn't want him to end up that way as well. It was bound to happen if we stayed together.

I choose a quiet time to share bits, and pieces of the nightmare I lived. I needed him to know about my monsters. I began by telling him that if it was too much for him, I would understand. I needed to tell him quickly before I lost my nerve. I was scared that it would change his feelings toward me to feelings of pity, or even disgust. If he was going to leave me, it had to be quick. I wanted to get it over with before any more time passed; before I got involved any deeper.

I relayed only the most basic details of what happened to me. I felt his body tense as he listened in silence. I watched for any sign of emotion as I spoke. As my story unfolded the reaction that registered on his face was not what I expected. The muscles twitched in his jaw, his fists clenched up, and his body stiffened. Then, he looked at me. He saw the defeated look in my eyes and all traces of anger fled from him. He enveloped me in an embrace, as if he wanted to shield me from my own past. The quiet strength of his protective arms was overpowering. He peered into my eyes, into my soul, and lingered there; his face just inches from my own. I sensed he would move heaven and earth to cleanse my pain, right the injustice that had been perpetrated against me. He kissed me as if he meant to make up for my life of hurt. I returned his kiss with a hunger that surprised us both. I pulled him to me feverishly, wanting him more than I ever wanted anyone in my life. He pulled his hungry mouth a breath away, and waited for me to open my eyes. When I opened them, he was looking at me again. He dropped a tiny kiss on my upturned nose, smiled tenderly, took my hand, and said he wanted to make sure I was ready before went any further.

That night, we found ourselves sharing my bed. It didn't cause him to run. He was incredibly sweet. He was careful, gentle, and made sure there was a soft glow in which I could see his sweet face and gazed into his eyes. His touch was tender and loving. He kissed me as if he meant to take my pain away. I pulled him to me anxiously, with a hunger, a need, I never felt before. Ever so tenderly, his fingertips brought on a stir of heat as my body shook at his every touch.

He laid me down as his mouth met mine, it was so soft, filled with an unyielding passion I was anxious to fulfill. We molded together as if we were the perfect pieces to a magical puzzle--meshing together to make us one. His skillful caress brought quakes to my body as I shuddered in pure delight. I writhed with pleasure at his affectionate kiss, yearning with pleasure as his body entered mine. My womanhood flowed with moisture as he rocked, slowly and gently. I gasped as my body arched up to meet him, taking everything he had, pulling him closer. His constant gaze never left my face as the heat of passion stirred us both into a frenzy of lovemaking. My body trembled as my own orgasms came. His body quivered with his own release. We laid in bed, molded together as if our bodies were made to fit exactly. I ran my hands over him, trying to memorize each part of him. Our lovemaking was pure perfection. I wanted the memory of that night embedded in my mind forever. He smiled lazily and pulled me closer to him. It was wonderful, and my heart felt complete.

We were inseparable after that night. Kayden made it

SHATTERED PANE

his mission to shower me with attention, and he catered to my want or need. He spoiled me constantly. We ate dinner at nice restaurants, went to movies, concerts and carnivals; smiling and laughing the whole time. He made me feel so special. Like a woman worthy of a king.

I couldn't shed the nagging fear that I would never be able to be the person he needed. He was so innocent, and I so jaded. He loved me so easily. It wasn't complicated for him. I began to realize that I loved him. I loved him more than I could ever love a man in my life, and for that, I wanted to protect him from me. I may have survived savage storms up to this point, but the cloud of my past always remained with me. It saddened my heart to think about sharing my dark cloud with him. The debris of my past intruded on even the most sacred parts of our relationship. I still occasionally experienced panic attacks I couldn't control. It was incredibly difficult to tell Kayden that I might have a panic attack at any point during sex, and that I needed the light on so I would know it was him there with me, not my demons.

I carried a lot of baggage from the abuse of my monsters, and the abandonment of my soon to be ex-husband. How could I pull this incredible man into my totally screwed up life? He had no idea what he was walking into. As much as I wanted to give my whole heart to him, I wasn't even a free woman yet. Ray still refused to sign the divorce papers, essentially holding me hostage by his irresponsible whims. He even fancied himself in love with me again, and asked me to take him back. What a joke! All I wanted was to shed his last name, and move on with my life.

Kayden and I grew closer, despite my reservations. He

JENNA K. SCOTT

had an uncanny knack for reading my emotions. Whenever he sensed I was slipping into doubt, he pulled me close and reminded me how much he cared for me. He refused to let my past become a blockade to any future we might have.

Chapter 23

Peeping Tom

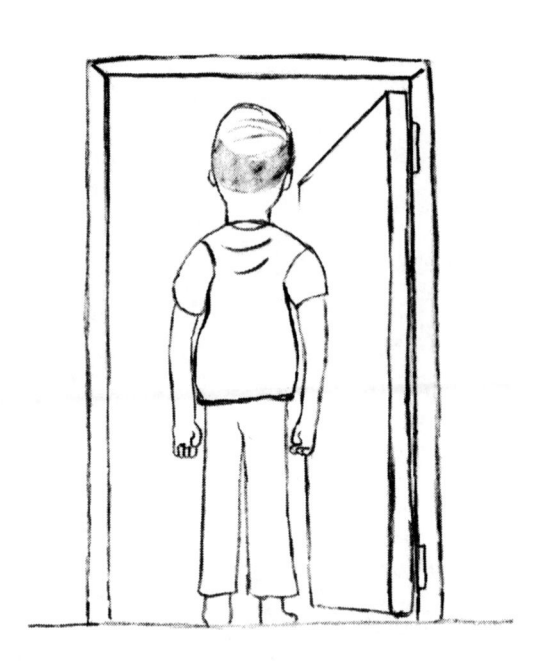

The demons I fought continued to penetrate their way into my new life; the biggest demon of all reared its ugly head once again. Grandpa Greg was sick. He need round the clock care as our family was called in to help.

I tried to take my turn in helping with my grandfather. I thought I could handle it, and I needed closure of some sort to heal my heart. The hatred I harbored for that man was like a mold that festered; it had grown for thirteen years. He destroyed parts of my soul for all eternity. I wanted to be free to give and receive love again. I felt like I needed to scrape some of the darkness out of my heart to do that; I couldn't carry it there any longer. Then maybe, just maybe, my heart could learn to expand and grow. Grow big enough to hold Kayden within it. I thought it was time to make amends; I would try to forgive my monster...my grandfather, but I could never forget.

Against my mother's wishes, I decided to take the night shifts, so I could keep my schedule at work and school. Plus, he would be sleeping so I wouldn't actually have to look at him much. I slept in the guest room, in hospital bed that Grandma Eden had died in. I went to bed fully clothed and on guard. I needed to leave the door open so I could hear if he called for me.

The first few nights came and went without incident. I heard him get up to use the restroom, and listened for the shuffle as he made it back to bed safely. The next night I heard him in the restroom, but I never heard him go back to bed. He left the bathroom quietly, but no shuffling of his feet to his room.

I felt as if someone was watching me, and for an instant

I was eight years old again and had to choke back the vomit that was creeping up my throat. Only then did I hear him return to bed. I was unable to sleep the rest of the night, haunted by the memories of his torture. I wondered how he slept, knowing what he had done to me. Each night for the next few nights I couldn't escape the feeling that he watched me on his return trip from the bathroom. I kept telling myself that it was my imagination and refused to look to the doorway.

By the end of the week, I was exhausted and decided to confront my anxiety that the old man watched me still. I laid down in bed, not turned away from the door, but looking directly at it. I needed to see what he was doing after he left the restroom. His routine was like clockwork.

As usual, I heard his door open, as he made his way to the restroom. After the flush of the toilet, I carefully placed the blanket so I could see out, but he wouldn't notice I was watching. I waited patiently, still. I heard the shuffle of the old man's unsteady gate, and then it stopped. There he stood, in my doorway, watching me as I pretended to sleep. He took two steps in and stopped. Just like the years before, he was as quiet as a mouse. My stomach felt sick as I squirmed, fighting the urge to bolt, clenching my jaw. In an instant I knew that if he took one step closer I would kill him. I wasn't the same defenseless little girl anymore. He would never spill my blood, or his seed in me again. He would not overtake me again. His decrepit body would not withstand the murderous rage I would unleash upon it if he attempted to touch me. I waited, ready to attack. If that son-of-a-bitch took one more step, it would be his last. He turned away, and returned to his room. The next day I bailed out. Eight months later my evil grandfather died in his sleep from cardiac arrest. His heart was so black I couldn't believe he held out that long. I found it ironic that a person as wonderful as my Grandma Eden would suffer a long painful death. Yet, this monster died peacefully in his sleep. Life could life be so cruel.

The funeral was nowhere near the size of my Grandmothers. He wasn't well liked. A few people were crying around us, but both Mom, and I could hardly keep from smiling. We went to make sure the bastard was truly dead. We needed the closure of witnessing his body being buried, deep in the earth.

Even from the grave, he managed to screw us. Grandma had a will made out so that all their possessions were equally divided among all her children, including Aunt Dina. She passed away first, so my grandfather instructed my Uncle Garrett to change the will. It excluded my mother, Landon, and my Aunt Dina. My grandfather was declared mentally incompetent years before, so because he was not of sound mind, legally he was not allowed to make that decision. However, Uncle Garrett took it upon himself to have it changed to only include the three remaining children.

No one can possibly understand the hurt this has caused. The ones in the will were the first ones allowed in the house to choose what they wanted for keepsakes. By the time Mom, Landon, and Dina were allowed in, most of it was gone. My mother and Uncle Landon were the most in need. Landon was told by my grandfather that if he announced he believed him and took his side, he would be put back into the will. Landon refused. The money is not what hurt them. It was the fact that her own siblings could so harshly stab them in the back.

As my family fell apart around me, I continued seeing Kaden a few days a week, and we enjoyed many long and remarkable nights together. He continued to be my protector and helped me tremendously by getting financial situations fixed. Ray screwed up our credit so badly I couldn't finance a stick of gum. I still hadn't successfully acquired a divorce, and Kayden helped me with that nasty little problem as well. He even went to court with me two out of the three hearings. He continued to be too good to be true. He was so perfect – and I was so screwed up. I was in no position to offer him anything but trouble, but he refused to leave. He continued to treat me like a princess, and with each compliment he showered upon me, he lifted my spirit a little higher. He built my confidence, gave me strength; he gave me a reason to try and a purpose to live. He taught me that it was ok for me to be happy. I began to allow myself to feel emotions that were once reserved only for fairy tales. I even began to think it possible my own fairy tales might come true.

My best friend Amy and her fiancé, Rob, were getting married. It was so exciting; I loved weddings. Celebrating Brittney and Jerry's wedding the year before was a blast. We had so much fun together, having our hair done, nails fixed, picking out dresses, and parties all around. Her wedding was beautiful, and the reception was unbelievable. We ate, drank, and danced the entire night long. Completely unforgettable.

Amy and Rob asked if I would be their maid of honor. I was overjoyed to have such a significant role in their wedding. Kaden had become close to them over the last year.

They asked him to be an usher, which made it twice as fun. It was a little tricky though, because the couple wanted Ray to be a groomsman. Knowing how close Rob and Ray were, I wasn't going to be the one who stood in the way of their choice of attendants. Besides, we were all adults. We should be able to work together and get along.

When the wedding day arrived. I wasn't prepared for the rush of feelings that hit me when I saw Ray. It was a combination of love, loathing, friendship, and hatred. I worked hard to keep those feelings at bay, and the wedding went off without a hitch. When it came time for pictures, we loaded the bus with beer, and headed to a secret location, sure create beautiful photos. We headed to a beautiful carousel at Fortune Park. I sat next to the driver since I held the directions, and I was the only one besides the newlyweds who knew where we were going. This turned out to be a bad idea. He couldn't seem to keep his eyes on the road, or his hands off my thigh. My friend Bryan, one of the groomsmen came to my rescue and took over giving directions. I looked for a spot to sit, and the only seat available was right next to Ray. I reluctantly sat beside him, perched awkwardly off to one side so I didn't accidentally touch him. Bryan quickly fixed it so I could sit with Kaden. I could feel Ray's eyes on me, but I had no idea what he was thinking. We finally pulled into Fortune Park. I jumped up, and was the first one off the bus. I used the excuse that I needed to go over the final arrangements with the photographer.

The photographer decided to do couple's shots, and both Ray and Kaden wanted their picture with me. Ray argued that legally I was still his wife, and Kaden loudly cited that

I would soon be his wife (which caught me by surprise). I backed up and declared that I was not having my picture taken with either of them. Neither of them argued, but eyed each other in a hateful silence.

The reception started, and I was determined to have a good time, despite the fact that Ray semi-stalked me throughout the night. Kayden mingled with the crowd, but never ventured too far from me, and always kept Ray in his sights. Ray did maneuver enough to get close to me for a moment. Long enough to tell me he didn't understand what I saw in Kayden, and he let me know, under no uncertain terms, that he was not the right man for me. Ray was hurt and confused, because I refused to stop the divorce proceedings. He thought I would run back into his cheating arms at the first sight of him, apparently. He abandoned me; left me to pick up the pieces of my shattered heart. I was angry that he expected me to give him a second chance, and even angrier that I considered it for brief moment. I felt a wide range of emotions that night, including sorrow that I hurt Ray by not taking him back. I loved him first, and even though he was not for me, I knew what a good person he could be. I didn't want to cause him more pain.

Kayden's parents were there also, and when they noticed the distressed look on my face, they quickly ushered me away to safety. I snapped back into reality and was grateful to be rescued. We moved along without as much as a backward glance at Ray. He got the hint and didn't bother me anymore. The rest of the evening passed without incident, and everyone enjoyed the remainder of the reception. Good food, good music and great friends made for a fantastic party. I watched the newlyweds as they gazed happily at each other during their first dance, not noticing anyone else in the room. I wondered if they would ever know how much I looked up to them as an example of what a passionate, loving marriage should be. Rob would move heaven and earth to make Amy smile, and she would do the same for him. Their love came so easily; naturally.

Kaden and I held each other close, dancing to all the slow songs. My heart tingled with a shimmer of a fantasy that we may have our own wedding someday. I had not entertained the idea until he mentioned it at the Carousel earlier that day.

Kaden stayed with me that night. We didn't need to talk about what happened with Ray. I don't know how he understood, because I didn't understand it myself, but Kaden knew me well enough to know that hurting Ray hurt me also. The fact that he deserved it didn't ease the unyielding ache in my heart. We continued our relationship as if nothing happened. I knew in my heart that Kaden always had my back.

He helped me overcome a lot of my fears and anxieties that hung on from my past. He listened when I needed to talk, lent me a strong shoulder when I needed to cry, and offered words of wisdom when they were warranted. The gentle stroke of his hand on the small of my back or a tender kiss from him was all I needed to get me through the day.

After almost two years, my divorce became finalized, and I was legally a free woman. Ray understood there was nothing left between us and signed all the papers. It was like a huge burden was lifted, and I felt free to give my heart to Kaden. This was a huge accomplishment, a day for celebrating.

It was a little surreal. In that moment of victory, I released my mind, wandered through all the events that passed, and it dawned on me how much support I had from my friends and family. I couldn't have gotten through it without my mom and my friends. They were the ones who helped me the most through the tough times. They listened to my rants, talked me down off the ledge a few times, and held my hair as I vomited from binge drinking and drugging. They cursed my demons with me, and distracted me from the bad stuff, so I could look into the future with hope. They helped me get to where I was stronger, more capable of managing my life, and gave me the gift of positive dreams.

Chapter 24

Peace

My fears of being with Kaden subsided. Our relationship continued strong and unwavering. I was working in the Microbiology lab, when he received two great offers for positions in his field of study. One job was in town, but the one he wanted was two hours away in Arkansas. Two hours! He had to make a decision. I knew it was a great opportunity for him, and I didn't want to influence his decision in any way. He was anxious to get out on his own, but that meant moving away. He moved back in with his parents after college, and never had his own place. Being married and divorced, I'd already lived on my own, and wanted him to have that opportunity too. Kaden had a supportive family, and they discussed his options at length. They asked how I fit into the picture, and he informed them he planned to ask me to move away with him.

I had never lived that far away from my mom, and had no desire to – ever. We were closer than any mother and daughter I knew. She was my lifeline, and I was hers. I knew in the back of my mind it would have to happen sometime in my life. The thought scared me incredibly.

Kaden took the job in Arkansas and moved into a small one bedroom apartment. I asked him to start up there without me for one year. I wanted him to know what it felt like to have his own space and manage it on his own. I felt as though it was the one thing he needed to experience before adding me, as a roommate, to the mix.

We maintained a long distance relationship for a year, seeing each other on the weekends. I went down there as much as possible, and he came home whenever he could. We squeezed every moment of happiness out of the time we had together. It was hard. I was greedy and wanted him all the time. The lab I worked in merged into one big lab, and my position was cut from the list. I moved upstairs in the hospital and worked with hospice care. It was a great job, but incredibly sad. It was hard having death all around me, and I could feel the depression setting in. Things were going well for Kaden though, and he moved into a new two bedroom apartment, to make room for me when I was ready to come.

Kaden began to make friends, both at work and in the apartment complex. There was a young couple upstairs, whom Kaden considered pretty good friends, but they constantly fought. One day she threw all her boyfriend's stuff out of the window, and kicked him out. Kaden and Emily began to hang out on occasion, breaking away from the loneliness of their empty apartments. I think that was the time I started getting jealous, and I was losing my mind at work. I was worried about the time they spent together. She was young, small, and beautiful. I was the girlfriend who told him to find his own way in the world.

He knew I was jealous of her, because I told him. Kaden found it silly and irrational, but it didn't change how I felt. The pull of my heartstrings were stronger than my ties to home, so off I went to keep the man I loved so dearly. I moved out of my mom's basement and into his apartment. Mom assured me she would be okay without me there. She knew I would come home on a moment's notice or be there if she needed me.

I was never comfortable with living with someone. There were too many variables that could go wrong. We weren't ready financially to make a forever trip down the aisle, but we both knew it would happen someday. So the night I moved in, we sat on the floor with my family Bible in hand, and swore ourselves as a faithful couple under the eyes of God. We weren't married, but it was the closest I could get.

I had a hard time finding any positions in a lab, much less in the Microbiology field. I always considered nursing, but it was never my first choice. Memorial Hospital had positions open for Certified Nurse's Aides. They paid for their employees to take the classes at the hospital, and gave on-the-job training. It didn't pay much, but at least I would have a job with some money coming in. It was definitely a huge step down from my previous position. None the less, I received my certificate, and took a position on the surgical floor.

Although I loved helping the patients, I quickly learned that nursing was not for me. I continued my position, but was lucky enough to work for the Medical Examiner, Frank, who took me under his wing. On nights we were not busy on the floor and Frank had a case, I was requested to work in the autopsy room as his aide. It was scary at first, but I loved being there to see all the human organs up close and personal. It was amusing to describe my experiences in a morgue to outside people. Their expressions ranged from intrigue to disgust. It never bothered me. I was amazed by the human body, and I got to see all the all the intricate details of how all the parts and pieces were put together. I learned a lot from him, and will forever be grateful.

I continued to have issues with my ovaries, and the endometriosis was hard. I was in pain a lot, and had several surgeries to remove cysts and scar tissue. Kaden loved me, and cared for me when I was sick. He was the most attentive nurse I have ever had. That lucky boy was never sick. He had allergies that would flare up, but never even called into work sick except for his back. He was so perfect in so many ways.

We made plans to take a weekend vacation to Chicago. It was a trip I was eager to take. We set up the dates, rented an RV, and made out plans for our weekend vacation. Unfortunately, I was sidelined by a trip to the ER, and yet another surgery to remove a ruptured cyst from my ovary.

I was so disappointed, and tired of being sick. Nothing ever seemed to work out in my favor. I wondered if Kaden was getting tired of taking care of me. I held doubts of ever making it to Chicago, I just knew something in my life would go wrong. My body had been battered so extensively as a child, I had to wonder if my medical issues were partially a result of the sexual abuse.

A couple months later, our mini vacation actually worked out. We drove up to Chicago. We stayed in an RV park that had an incredible view of the small lake. There was a small little inlet that held a tall beautiful tree. The next day we went to Six Flags, met some friends for dinner, and saw an old time drive in double feature on the way home. On the way back to the RV, we stopped at a little stand that was still selling fruit late into the night. We picked out some cherries, fruit for breakfast, and continued back.

It was around 2:00 am when we arrived at the RV. We unloaded the food we bought and quickly put it away. Kaden wanted to take a walk down by the lake. I was less than enthusiastic about coming back with a million mosquito bites; sweaty from the heat and humidity. Kaden persuaded me with a few kisses placed on the hollow of my neck, and before long he could have taken me anywhere he wanted. Besides, it was his vacation too, and I would do anything I could to make him happy.

He loved the tree that stood out of nowhere as we made that our destination. Kaden was quiet along the way. We were captivated by the beauty of the lake. The moonlight cast a glow off the water, it was a magnificent sight, and I enjoyed the peaceful silence of the night. When we reached the lake, we paused under the big tree that was there. Up close it was beautiful. The smell of hay, and wood filled the air around us. The bark laid perfect against the tree, as I gently patted it, and the branches lay silently over our heads. The lake water was still, and the grass was a freshly cut. We took a few minutes just to take in the world that surrounded us. Nothing but pure nature laid ahead of us.

He took my hand and looked at me. His eyes glistened in the moonlight as he gazed into my eyes, as if he was peering into my soul. He slowly dropped down on one knee, hands shaking, and asked me to marry him. In his hand was the most beautiful ring I ever saw; a stunning princess cut engagement ring. I was extremely elated, and quickly told him yes. I wanted us to start out even so I also got down on one knee also, and cried as I wrapped my arms around him in snug embrace. The only thing I knew right then and there, was that I loved him with all my heart, and I didn't want to let go. We went back to the RV, popped open a bottle of Champaign, and feasted on chocolate covered strawberries and cherries. I was in heaven.

I couldn't help but to admire my ring; waving my hand so the diamond sparkled in the moonlight. He had it custom made as an original piece. It boasted a one carat diamond in the middle, a swirl of baguette diamonds on each side, followed by an inlay of circle diamonds descending in size down the sides. It was fantastic, my heart fluttered with disbelief, and astonishment.

We made love with unrestraint, each of us giving ourselves to the other fully, completely. As we held each other close, sleep came soundly, and easily. I felt safe, and warm as his heart beat gently put me to sleep. Through the night, a storm developed, and it began to rain. I loved listening to the slight pitter patter on the tin roof. It lulled me back to sleep.

When we woke up the next morning, the pillows, sheets, and mattress were all soaked with water. There was a tiny hole in the RV, and during the storm water had leaked onto the bed. We glanced at each other, and busted out laughing at the soggy mess we were in. Nothing could dampen our spirits that morning. We moved to a dry spot in the RV, and celebrated our engagement once again.

After our return home, we called everyone we knew to announce our engagement. It was exciting; I felt as though I reached the highest honor known to man. We decided to buckle down, save every penny we made for the wedding, and a down payment on a house. Kaden's parents gave us a monetary engagement gift to help. It was incredibly considerate of them, and I was happy to have them in my life. I loved planning the wedding; it was incredibly stressful getting things in order from 200 miles away.

If there was one thing I knew about myself, it's that I wanted children desperately. Kaden was open to starting a family right away, but we both knew it would be difficult, if not impossible for me to conceive. We searched for a doctor who would try to help our dreams come true. The excitement was overwhelming when we found one that could.

My gynecologist wanted to try a new drug to heal my endometriosis and give us a chance of having a baby of our own. Now that I knew Kayden was ready for a baby too, I couldn't get pregnant quick enough. We planned our wedding for September 19, 1999; the estimated date I could conceive on this medication. We hoped and prayed to get pregnant on our honeymoon. First, we had a few hurdles to overcome to prepare my womb to conceive. Surgery was performed to remove as much of the endometriosis as possible. They were unable to remove much due to the fact it adhered itself to my kidneys, bladder, as well as my reproductive system.

I started receiving shots weekly, putting me into a chemically induced menopause. It stopped my ovaries from working, so the estrogen would stop feeding the endometriosis. I was in full-blown menopause with every single symptom possible. There were days I just knew Kaden was going to walk out the door for work and never come back. He handled my craziness like a champ though, and we made it through.

Our weekend trips and scheduled days off were used for the two hour trip home, to complete the list needed for the wedding. The ceremony was arranged, and set up. The biggest issue was my bridesmaids' dresses. Most of our wedding party was either pregnant, ready to give birth, or recently had a baby. Their bodies were constantly changing, and money was tight as their families started to grow. So we agreed on a shorter dress, and would use the same fabric and pattern, so it could easily be adjusted to fit their needs.

I went to my appointment in June to gauge my hormones. The medication needed to be adjusted occasionally so it could work with my body to its fullest potential. To our surprise, my levels were perfect for conception, so we stopped the drug three months prior to our wedding. We were advised to start trying right away. It baffled me; the fact that I could be pregnant on our wedding day, intentionally. We started to monitor my ovulation cycle, and received a whole lot of fun on those days.

We continued with the wedding plans, and the final details were falling into place. My co-ed wedding shower was hosted by my Matron of Honor, Amy, and my best friend, Brittany. It was held under a pavilion in the park. We had one huge party; it was the best co-ed wedding shower I had ever been to. Amy was incredibly close to giving birth to her second child. She was completely filled with the baby that would arrive shortly. I rubbed her swollen belly, and dreamed of the day I would feel the movement of my own child in my womb.

A week before the wedding, I was nervous, and had my doubts. Not about Kaden, but about myself. All of my insecurities rushed at me like a speeding bullet, and I felt as though I would explode any moment. I was afraid of letting Kaden down constantly, and was unsure how I would fit in his life as a lover, wife, and hopefully, a mother. Was I good enough for him? Could I handle it again if he grew tired of me, and discarded our marriage like a worn out dish rag? I knew he loved me, but did he love me enough to last for all eternity? Unanswered questions raced through my mind, faster than I could keep up.

Three days before, he sat me down for a talk. He knew me like the back of his hand, and must have noticed my anxiety. He informed me that he loved me with all his heart and soul and couldn't wait to make me his wife. That if I had any doubts, I should voice them now. I shared with him how I felt; he expressed to me that he was only marrying once, and it would be for life. He wanted desperately for me to be his wife. He would be committed to our wedding vows, and would follow through with them throughout our lives.

After he left, I started to panic even more. I already had one failed marriage under my belt. What if I fell short again, and failed him? All my doubts were about myself. None about him or how much I loved and respected him. I knew we would have our share of obstacles to overcome. Yet, I was unsure if I held the capability to hold it together. I was positive with Ray, thought we could survive anything, and the result of that experience almost killed me. I was wrong then, what if I was wrong again? I kept to myself for a few days, not wanting to share my distress with Kaden. I examined our relationship from every angle, dissecting it like I would a human heart. I evaluated the differences between my first marriage, and my upcoming one. I had to convince my intellectual mind it would be safe to follow my heart.

After three grueling days of laying out all the details, exploring my innermost feelings, I came to the conclusion that I was marrying him for every right reason in the book. The one big difference is the fact that I wasn't blinded by love, but I was going into it with my eyes, and heart wide open. My love for Kaden wasn't skewed by the rose-colored glasses I refused to take off during my first marriage. I loved Kaden completely, faults and all; although there weren't many. I was ready to give him all I had to offer.

They day had come for me to marry my best friend, and the love of my life. It started with showers, hairdos, and make up. It felt like it was going by incredibly fast, and I was missing each step as it happened. I started to look around at my beautiful wedding party, hair elegantly done, and in their magnificent royal blue dresses. I took snapshots with my mind, and committed them to my memory. These were the things I never wanted to forget.

I chained smoked outside our dressing room door, trying to gain control of my trembling legs so I could walk steadily down the aisle. It wasn't helping. My dad came in to see me concealing a flask of whiskey in his pocket. It wasn't something I could throw back, but was enough to calm my nerve racking anxiety. For those drinks, I was incredibly grateful. I asked my friend's to peek outside the door to check on Kaden. I wondered if he was half as nervous as I was. He was not. He was as happy as could be, greeting our guests, and twirling Alana in circles. She loved how her dress would swing out in a twirl around her.

The music began as we all took our respective places. I reminded myself of all the rules to follow--keep breathing, and don't lock your knees. It was silly that I reminded myself to breathe, it was a normal function, yet that day it was extremely difficult. I stayed hidden from the door as they were slowly opened to allow the wedding party in. Bridesmaids first, followed by Amy, pulling a decorated wagon holding her son Dalton, and Brittney's son Trey. They were incredibly cute in their little tuxedos, sitting tolerantly waiting for the ride.

Alana was right in front of me, holding her basket, and gently delivering her rose petals down the aisle in her own little grace and style. I could tell she felt like a fairy princess with all eyes on her. She was delightful, like a breath of fresh air. The doors were closed, and I was ushered to my starting point. I was shaking horribly.

We made the decision in the beginning that both of us would walk half way down, and we would meet on equal ground, in the middle. My parents already gave me away once; I wanted to give myself to him of my own free will. Slowly, the doors were opened. I stood there in my lace candlelight wedding gown, veil over my face, trying to will my feet to move. They felt frozen, and incapable of movement.

The wedding planner placed her hand on my back, with a small shove I was walking, barely. My eyes never left Kaden, and I could see the relief flow from him as we started the walk towards each other. I couldn't feel or notice anyone or anything around me, just the man I was about to marry in front of me. His face was tender, and sweet. When we met, I took his arm, and we continued toward the altar, together.

The Pastor asked us to kneel on the step in front of him. My body was unsteady, so I kept my hand on Kaden's arm for support, and apparently held the rail a little too tight. The Pastor made a joking comment about how I needed to loosen my grip before my hand lost all circulation. I blushed, removed my hand, and only returned it when I felt unsteady.

Our vows were read, the candles were lit, and roses were given to our mothers. We were pronounced husband and wife as we kissed for the second time, united under God. The shattered pieces of my heart were slowly restored. I may never be able to completely repair the window to my past, there were pieces destroyed, missing, and cracks that would forever remain. The few pieces that remained intact helped me envision the window to my future with some clarity and hope. It was clean and bright. Kaden was truly my knight in shining armor, who rescued me heart and soul.

Chapter 25

Heaven on Earth

It has been sixteen years since we took our oath and twenty years since we met. We have been blessed with two beautiful children, a girl and a boy. They are growing into little adults much faster than I ever believed. I have taken the time out, to take those snapshots in my mind. It gives me glorious memories when I am down. Restores my faith at their smiles, and no one could ever take them away. My husband provides for us, working hard every day. He is a wonderful father and an excellent husband.

It is hard to understand the issues I deal with on a day to day basis. That is okay, because I have still won the biggest part of the battle. I am here, with a family I love more than life itself.

I am perceived by some as naive and trusting. The truth is, I don't trust anyone with my whole entire heart. The worse pain comes from people I do trust, and loved the most. I will never be ready to feel that anguish again.

I now hold my family close to me. I have found my comfort in my children, husband, mother, and of course, the bright spots in my window pane. Yes, they will hurt me off and on. Unintentionally, just by growing up. I can and will get through the rough times and glorify in the good.

I can't say that our lives and relationship has remained smooth as honey. There have been points in which I felt isolated, and didn't want to continue on. Somehow, we have managed to move past them, by working together instead of apart. To not give up on each other. After all, we vowed before God, for richer or poorer, in sickness and health, in good times and bad, until death do us part. I made the right decision that day, and married the most wonderful man on earth.

About the Author

My ultimate goal for this book is to spread the word about how devastating abuse can be. Lives have been ruined, and even lost over these senseless tragedies. My one dream in life would to be able to start a safe-haven for victims of abuse. Buy some land, build a structure that could house at victims, and provide them with safety. I want it to hold everything victims would need in order to start the healing process. Including counselors and psychiatrists to aid in the journey. To be able to help everyone in the world, but I will start with whatever I have, and build from there. I will start with one person at a time.

Too many victims are overlooked, turned away, or don't have the strength of independence to get them started. I would like to give hope to the people who have none. There are more victims out there than you will ever know. Dark secrets hidden deep within them, unable to be freed. Scared to ask for help due to the possible repercussions they may face.

Thank You

A huge thank you to my **husband**, who has always stood behind me, has given me the space and time I needed to complete my life story. He has done his best over the years to understand my struggles, and has allowed me the space to base decisions off my own life's experience. I can never thank him enough for all he has given to me. I truly love him with all my heart; he is more than I ever dreamed of.

To my **children**, as they understood the importance of this "project" I have worked on. For understanding that this is for their future as well as mine. I hope they know that my intentions are always good, and I only hope to protect them from the evils of the world. They are my innocent souls. I want to make this a better world for them.

To my **family**, the ones who have gotten lost in this tangled web of life. To the ones whom he has hurt. I will always be here for you, to aid, and guide you when you are ready. For the ones who felt the pain and loss, and for those young enough to be free from the burden.

I am thankful for my **friends** whom have helped, and supported me while writing this book. It brought out emotions in me I didn't know I had. A huge thank you to one special friend, Bridget, for all your help. You have done an amazing job, and I could never thank you enough. I am so proud of you and everything you have accomplished. Both with me as a team, and without me as an individual.